Clarissa and the Poor Relations

Alicia Cameron

For Holly, Germaine and Anastasia and for those whom I imagined would have time to read it: my father Jack, my brothers Ray and Paul and especially my sister Pat. I can hear you all laughing.

Contents

Chapter 1

Clarissa Convinces

Looking down upon the curate's thinning hair from her vantage point of the library chair, Miss Clarissa Thorne felt herself to have borne enough.

'Do please rise, Mr Peterkin. I would myself if you hadn't quite caught yourself in my skirts,' she said tartly. She was quite a young lady, about eighteen summers, but with a determined chin set in a face surrounded by mousy ringlets caught up carelessly in a rather tattered ribbon. She wore a plainly cut black muslin, as befitted her mourning state. She might have been passably pretty had she not had a quite unladylike air of certainty in her large grey eyes.

The Reverend Mr Peterkin rose at once and was about to deliver himself of a lecture as to the tones young ladies should adopt when speaking to members of the clergy, when he recollected that this would not forward his case.

'Indeed, Miss Thorne, it is only my sincere intention to throw myself at your feet, to act as your solace, your comforter in this harsh world that caused me to...' But his companion had already pulled a decrepit bell chain and was holding out her hand to bid him farewell in an unmistakable fashion.

'I am obliged to you for your charitable sentiments, sir, but you have now received your answer and must take your leave.'

As Mr Peterkin grasped her hand automatically, he felt he was losing control of the situation. He gulped and said, 'But Miss Thorne, you cannot have considered your position, your parents both dead ... you need a man to guide you ...'

She withdrew her hand and looked past him at her superior servant.

'Ah, Sullivan, here is Mr Peterkin taking his leave of us, please show him out,' she said, with the utmost cheerfulness.

'Certainly, Miss,' said the impassive Sullivan, holding the door as the curate left the room in some disorder. As they descended the stairs, Mr Peterkin stared with dislike at Sullivan's back. How Mrs Thorne's Academy for Young Ladies had ever merited a servant who gave himself such superior airs as Sullivan was a mystery to most in the county, but not to the curate. When Viscount Ashcroft's daughter had married mere Mr Thorne, a writer and free thinker and a younger son to boot, the first footman of the Ashcroft estate had accompanied her to her new home bringing with him such an elegance of manner as to terrify the local gentry but to reassure the parents of the young ladies who were educated there.

'I beg your pardon, sir, for the circumstance of you finding yourself ushered into Miss's presence alone. Might you tell me which of the servants should have done such a thing?' Whenever Sullivan alluded to the other servants, he did so with the air of one still presiding over a multitude instead of the cook, parlour maid and groom that was all that the house boasted beyond term time.

Mr Peterkin was jamming on his hat hurriedly and had the grace to blush. 'Well, as to that ... I let myself in through the garden door ... as I wished to offer ... religious comfort at this time of mourning for Miss Thorne.'

'Indeed, sir?' Sullivan's eyebrows raised a little at this and Mr Peterkin, knowing himself to be the butler's social superior – why he should feel a wish to explain himself. 'Perhaps you will allow me to announce you next time Sir, and then you would find Miss properly accompanied by one of the other ladies.'

'Well, yes. But if you wish to infer ... It is not your place, Sullivan to .... A clergyman's case is very ... Good day.'

'And good day to you, my slimy weasel done up in a clerical collar,' said Sullivan after he closed the door behind him, 'and a good riddance to you. And if it's not my place to be guarding my young lady from the likes of you, I don't know whose it is.'

Clarissa meanwhile had thrown herself into an adjoining room, wherein lay three ladies variously occupied in packing up the contents of the room.

'That's it,' she said imperiously as she entered the room. Her eyes were flashing and her cheeks flushed, and she looked quite arresting despite her dull gown.

A lady of some forty-five years in an unbecoming round dress of mud--coloured cambric looked up from her employment of sorting through piles of dusty books and said, 'My dear Clarissa, whatever can have upset you?'

'I have just had to suffer the impertinence of an offer from Mr Peterkin, so now you will all *have* to listen to me,' Clarissa declared. She moved a work box from a red velveteen chair and sat down whilst with exclamations of astonishment her companions abandoned their tasks and joined her, two sitting on the sofa and the other on the footstool by her chair, chafing her hands to soothe her evident agitation.

The ladies on the sofa could not have provided a greater contrast. True, both were dressed in sober grey gowns, made up at the neck and free of any softening touches such as lace or the sad knots of ribbon with which the third lady had sought to relieve the severity of her attire. But then Miss Appleby, seated at Clarissa's feet, was of a romantical disposition, and she still held a faint flame alight for the gentleman who might one day seek her hand. That this gentleman was very late in appearing, no one could doubt. The other two ladies would have scorned such hopes. Therein lay their only similarity.

Miss Oriana Petersham was without doubt a beauty of the first water, and though she pulled back her golden hair severely and simply pinned it in a loop at her neck she could not help the little ringlets that escaped to frame her heart-shaped face, the darker lashes that curled around her large green eyes, or the perfection of her pert nose and bow-shaped mouth. It did her no good either to wear the sober unadorned gown, which served only to act as a foil to her magnificent figure and beautiful face. That face at the moment wore an expression of great concern, for too often had the beautiful Oriana Petersham been the object of unsolicited male attentions for her to be anything but unsympathetic to Clarissa's ordeal.

Alongside her sat a lady probably fifteen years her senior at thirty-five, her figure as stolid as her companion's was lithe, her complexion as ruddy as Oriana's was delicate, her hair as dark and straight as was the other's pale and curled. Her brows were dangerously close to meeting over her determined brown eyes, but her face was so impassive that it was hard to know how she had taken Clarissa's outburst. Miss Augusta Micklethwaite's face did not betray her thoughts.

Miss Appleby, her grey and brown ringlets (owing a great deal to a hot iron) bouncing thinly about her face as she agitatedly chafed at Clarissa's hand, 'Oh, how can this be ... Mr.Peterkin, so romantic. To have harboured a *tendre* for you all this time ... I should never have guessed ... Indeed, I always thought that he disliked you, Clarissa, for do you not remember how he scolded you over that button that you put in the poor box ... But that was quite some time ago now ...' She broke off in agitation as Clarissa withdrew her hand.

'*Tendre.* You can scarce be serious,' uttered Clarissa. Her anger gave way to a giggle at the memory of Mr Peterkin's obsequiousness.

Miss Micklethwaite said in her plain northern voice, 'He has heard about the inheritance, of course. You are a fool Louisa.'

Miss Appleby was too used to Miss Micklethwaite's unfurbished mode of conversation to take offence at this statement. 'Oh he would not ... I'm sure ... But how could he?' she finished, and her watery eyes were bright with agitation. What was once a frail beauty was now a scrawny but wirier face and a figure with a resilience borne of hardship in the service of various households as a drudge-governess until her last five years of bliss as a teacher at the Academy that her old school friend had established. Here she had been coddled, she thought, treated with real respect by dear Clarissa's mama, now sadly dead.

'I should imagine that it has something to do with Jane ...' Oriana saw that Miss Appleby was still looking confused and explained. 'Our cook, Jane is second cousin to Lottie, the parlour maid at the vicarage.'

'Servants know everything,' exclaimed Miss Appleby.

'Mr Peterkin said that he was wishful to marry me to give comfort to a motherless waif,' said Clarissa, her voice tragic.

Oriana's eyes danced, 'He never did. And I always thought him a man of no address.'

'Well it is not funny. And when I asked him if he was in a position to support a wife ...'

'Oh, Clarissa, you did not,' interjected Miss Appleby, in shocked accents.

'Well, I did. I said I did not scruple to ask him such a question since I had no parents to ask it for me,' said Clarissa pertly, but with her eyes dancing quite as much as Oriana's, 'and he stammered and said that he did not at the moment have the means, but that if I should prove to have a little competence from my mamma, he believed that I would need a man of his experience to manage it for me. He gave himself away completely. Depend upon it, he has offered for me because he has heard of my cousin's death and my inheriting Ashcroft Manor.'

'I'm sure you must be correct,' said Oriana with sparkling eyes. 'What a ridiculous little man. He seeks to profit from an alliance with one to whom he has shown naught but impatience any time these last three years.'

'But surely he is correct, my dear Oriana. Clarissa *does* stand in need of guidance at this difficult time. A gentleman's strong shoulder, his decisive nature ...'

'Bah!' ejaculated Miss Micklethwaite impatiently, 'He cannot even decide between chicken or dressed crab for dinner. He can little pretend to have offered much in the way of support to Clarissa in these last months since her dear mamma has passed away. It is Mr Norbert who has behaved as a vicar should, even though we were all cast into the doldrums anytime his visit lasted above twenty minutes. If she needs guidance then no doubt her brother may offer it to her, even if he's as stiff-rumped a young longwind as you may meet in a twelvemonth.'

'Augusta,' said Miss Appleby, in a faint but pleading tone, 'you must not say such things of Mr Thorne. To be sure he is a man of high principles and strong views ...'

'Dearest Appleby, it is no more than my mother used to say, for try as she might she could never warm to her stepson. Even my father felt that he had adopted his air of outraged virtue only as a reaction to his and my mother's more liberal views. He could never bear to be thought of as different or *eccentric* as they were. Father blamed Harrow.' As Clarissa spoke her large eyes took on an affectionate twinkle as she thought of her parents, dead within a year of each other, united in Heaven as they had been in life. She sighed and looked at each of her friends in turn. 'You are quite right, however. John does mean to visit me on Monday, as he informs me in his letter. He further informs me that he has taken the liberty to visit Ashcroft and finds it in a very sorry state. He also advises me that he has set his lawyers on to sell it, there being no objection now that the succession is broken and the entail is ended, he is sure that will be my wish. As for the rest, he invites me to go and stay with him, where he is sure, *sure*, mind you, that I will be of help to Cornelia with the children.' For most of this speech, Clarissa had been wringing a lace handkerchief to death whilst pacing passionately about the room. 'I have been brought up to be of independent mind - can you *imagine* what my life would be in such a household? I should die.'

'I have often thought that your mother did not know what she did when she allowed you so much free rein in your thinking and behaviour. *Here* your education stood you in good stead, but out in the world people take a dim view of young ladies who set themselves up against men's opinions, or seek to take part in political debate. I spoke to her many times on this matter, but she did not expect to leave you unprotected so soon,' so said Miss Micklethwaite, whilst she wiped away what might have been a tear from her fierce eyes.

'Yes, but I have a plan. I shall not be here to listen to John's advice - for I shall be at Ashcroft. And all of you shall go with me.'

'But you cannot,' squeaked Miss Appleby.

'Clarissa, you cannot have considered,' said Miss Petersham.

'Dear Appleby, only listen. Of course I cannot go with no respectable female to accompany me, but with three of you we shall do splendidly. John can hardly object to the respectability of that.'

'I should rather think he would object to us hanging onto your coattails,' said Miss Micklethwaite roundly.

'Yes, and he'd be right. Take Miss Appleby, by all means, but there is no need to take on all of us. I could not be your pensioner at any cost,' declared the beautiful Miss Petersham, the flush on her face causing her to look even lovelier than normal.

'Do you wish to go and live with your brother who will try to sell you in marriage to the highest bidder again?' demanded Clarissa.

'I shall be there only long enough to find a new situation,' declared Oriana. 'Besides, he cannot force me.'

'But he can make life as unbearable for you as John can for me. You know that getting another position is unlikely. Finding this situation suited you, but you are far too beautiful to be accepted as a governess in most houses.'

Oriana bent her head and bit her lip. Clarissa leant forward and grasped her tightly clasped hands in both of her own.

'Would you not rather be of use to me?' she said pleadingly, 'Look, when Mamma died and we knew we had to close the school at the end of the year, all of us thought that we would need to part, to break up our cosy life here. Then, when my cousin died so unexpectedly, I thought I could use my inheritance to help us all.' She turned impulsively, 'Appleby, dearest, you do not really wish to go and live with your cousin

Farnham and all those dreadful little children, do you? You know that you'll be treated as an unpaid servant in that house. I remember the exhausted state you were in when you returned from there last summer.' Miss Appleby made inarticulate noises in faint protest. 'I truly need a companion, one who I can talk to of my mamma and papa and who understands me as well as you do. You would not abandon me?'

Miss Appleby took the badly used handkerchief from Clarissa's grasp and sobbed into it. 'Oh, my dear Clarissa - so kind ... if I could only be sure I would not be a burden to you ...'

Clarissa turned her burning eyes and determined young face to her other friends, not so easily moved as Miss Appleby.

'You have not thought, my dear Clarissa, what living in a house such as Ashcroft would entail. If your brother is right and the estate has been neglected then perhaps it is right to sell. Then you and Miss Appleby could set up your own establishment in Bath.' Oriana's honeyed voice sought to calm down Clarissa's spirits.

'You are correct in thinking that I do not know what running an estate entails - that is why I need *you* to show me, Oriana.'

Sir Ralph Petersham had involved his daughter in many male pursuits, riding roughshod over her mother's complaints. He had included her in all estate matters and she had proved so apt a pupil that he had left a deal of responsibility in her hands. When his son Fitzroy came home from Cambridge in the vacations, he was often adjured to "Ask Oriana what's what." When the young man had shied away from including Oriana in what he had felt to be his domain and had thus done something unwise, his father had trenchantly ordered, 'Leave it to your sister next time.' Sir Ralph had meant his beautiful daughter to be the wife of a great man, able to stand at his side as an equal, as his own wife had never done, and had he lived who knows what might not have happened.

As it was, a jealous brother had been the one to oversee Oriana's come-out in London, and he had been pleased to accept, on her behalf, an offer from an Earl who was both wealthy and approaching sixty. Oriana's disgrace in calling off her wedding and her brother's consequent anger had induced her to seek her position at Mrs Thorne's Academy. Her brother, still questioned by the world about the fate of his beautiful sister, had never forgiven her.

'Mother always said that Ashcroft was a prosperous estate at the time of my uncle, and my cousin has only owned it for five years. He was a sad rake and possibly a libertine but *surely* he could not have done so much harm in that time. Oriana, you could help me make it prosperous again. Don't you see, far from being a *tax* on me you can be a *real help* to me.'

Oriana's eyes sparkled then dulled again, 'If only I could, my dear. We do not know the people... they would have to come to *trust* us Clarissa, but with the help of a good agent ...' She tried to look in Clarissa's eyes, for signs of the charity that she would so deplore but saw only hope and determination. 'Oh, *could* we?' she said.

Clarissa leapt to her feet and danced Oriana to hers. 'My dear, so you'll come.' She and Oriana shrieked and danced about the room. Just as abruptly she stopped and turned to Miss Micklethwaite.

'Dearest Waity, you know that I shall need you to help me set the house in order.'

Miss Micklethwaite's frown became more terrible. 'You do not need me to feed as well.'

'For all my Greek and Latin, I have not learned any of the housekeeping things a lady should know, for how could dear Mamma teach me what she did not know herself? And we need you to scare away the dragons, Waity. Just *think* what attentions I might receive from mushrooms like the curate if I have not you by me to lend respectability. As for Oriana, you know we dare not send her out without she comes home followed by some smitten gentleman.'

A gasp from Oriana at this made Miss Micklethwaite smile sourly.

'And I should *so* value your support my dear Augusta,' said Miss Appleby gently, 'for in the absence of any gentleman, I cannot but feel you are the next best thing. 'Why, what can I have said to make you go into such transports of laughter, Clarissa, Oriana?'

But the young ladies were laughing so hard at the outrage on Waity's face that they had to grasp onto each other to keep upright. Miss Micklethwaite's forehead smoothed a trifle.

'I think, Louisa, that you and I will be needed to keep these two in check,' she said.

'Well, if you think so, Augusta, then of course we shall go,' said Miss Appleby in a confused voice.

'I do,' said Miss Micklethwaite, her grim voice repressing the unseemly levity of the young ladies, 'And what is more we had better go now to change for dinner. Perhaps I can find some knee breeches.'

'*Knee breeches?* Whatever can you mean?' said Miss Appleby to the retreating back of her friend. 'Girls?' she uttered vaguely. But it was no use, the two young ladies had collapsed in an unseemly heap onto the sofa, in helpless gales of laughter.

Later that evening, Clarissa sat in bed hugging her knees. A life with her brother and his wife was a bad enough thought, but she was determined that no such fate must touch her friends. She had seen too well the life of the despised poor relations, women who drudge for their families for a little more status than a maid and less money - for rare indeed was the family who took on the responsibility of a portionless female with any acceptance of equality. They must be grateful for the benefits of their position, the benefits which might include insult, humiliation and exhaustion from the performance of a hundred thankless tasks each day: the complete inability to order a second of one's own life. Even if she could bear it, her dear, dear, friends must not.

CHAPTER 2

The Ladies Contrive

If they were to quit the academy before the arrival of Mr Thorne, the ladies had a great deal to do. Miss Micklethwaite did venture the opinion that it would be better to await his arrival and inform him of her decision, but when Clarissa declared that it would be better if he were faced with a *fait accompli* she could not but see the force of it. A young man of overbearing manner who was ten years her senior, Mr Thorne would not take kindly to his wishes being overset. No doubt, thought Augusta, he also had some plans as to how to *manage* Clarissa's money for her: plans that might be to his advantage. Of this, she said nothing, merely marshalling the ladies in the packing.

They could now take all the books that they had been so unwilling to leave behind (even though *Basic Arithmetic for Young Scholars* was unlikely to be of use in a country house), for Sullivan had declared his intention of travelling ahead with the trunks, whilst Mary could accompany the ladies on the hired post chaise. This was a relief, for who knows what state the house would be in and Sullivan could be depended upon to provide the basic comforts for their arrival.

He had something to say to Clarissa before he left. 'You have not been wont to worry much about your mode of dress here miss, quite understandable, I'm sure. But it will not do to arrive in Hertfordshire looking, well ...' Sullivan paused, embarrassed.

'Shabby-genteel. I know,' said Clarissa. 'But there is hardly time ... I'll discuss it with the ladies. Thank you Sullivan.'

'Very good, ma'am.'

Oriana had already done some thinking about this she confided, when Clarissa brought up the subject. 'And I believe I have the very solution, if you will not take it amiss. Your mama's wardrobe and some chests of fabric that I found have given us some unexpected treasures. If you would not object to having her black silk evening gown altered for you, I should think that would be the very thing. Plus the two black muslin gowns that Mrs Trimble in town is making for you will be sufficient for daywear until we find someone in Hertfordshire.'

'Yes,' said Clarissa, blushing, 'But will they be grand enough for the lady of the manor? I wish to be taken seriously when I deal with the locals. I do not want feminine folderols, but only to at least look like a lady of quality rather than the silly schoolgirl that I fear I am.'

Oriana suppressed a sigh and grabbed at her hand. 'Only come with me and see what your mamma has been hiding.'

Upstairs in her mother's room were closets and chests that she had not explored since she was a child. Oriana had thrown them opens and had heaped the gorgeous contents onto the bed. Clarissa gave a little sigh at entering her mamma's sanctum, but soon became embroiled in the quite luminous hoard before her. Laid away carefully in mothballs and lavender, was all the finery of a Viscount's daughter that was useless for a provincial schoolteacher. To be sure, fashions of whale-boned bodices and crinoline skirts looked strange to the young ladies who wore the simpler styles, but the sheer luxury and colour of the silks, satins, brocades and gold net could not but delight them.

'Look. Some Brussels lace that we can use to trim your mourning gowns,' said Oriana, 'and a lace shawl from Spain to wear with your mamma's black silk in the evening. And when we get to Hertfordshire you will likely find a dressmaker to make the velvet of this cloak into riding habit. And if you were to buy some lengths of fine wool we can fashion a very respectable carriage dress and trim the bonnet and muff with this ermine.'

Clarissa fingered the strange clothes with confusion and delight. 'Trimmed with *ermine* ... oh no, Oriana. I just wished to look more respectable.'

'Stuff and nonsense,' cried Oriana stoutly; 'You must look the thing. You cannot well go into Hertfordshire looking like you have spent last winter counting the coals on the fire individually, however true it may be. You would not like your new neighbours to *pity* you, would you?'

'I should not,' exclaimed Clarissa, revolted by the idea, 'But what modes there were in Mamma's time! Very grand, of course. But Mother was such a bookish woman that it seems strange to think of her going to balls wearing such stuff as *this,*' she held up a purple satin gown with gold brocade overdress.

'Yes, very strange. One must suppose the colour was fashionable at the time. However, don't you think that we could quite easily cut it up to make an underdress and perhaps an evening cape for Miss Appleby? If we made a simple over dress of this lavender crepe it would be quite in keeping with her semi-mourning for your mama. And it would add little to your consequence to have your companion dressed as she is now.'

Looking at Oriana's delight, Clarissa believed that she must have missed the fashionable world more than she thought, and also that she had been itching to gown Clarissa for some time.

So the ladies devised their scheme to dress their elders in clothes more befitting their new station, and it seemed that it could all be done at very little cost with the aid of the riches in the late Mrs Thorne's chest. A fine dove-coloured muslin from Mamma's cupboard could be taken in several inches for Miss Appleby, along with a pelisse to match, which could very well be given a 'touch of *Paris*' (as Miss Petersham called it) by trimming it with some dark grey velvet ruched ribbon from one of the assorted dresses.

Miss Micklethwaite was more of a problem. It was useless to suppose she would allow herself to be done up in purple satin. She was, indeed, the daughter of a respectable solicitor who had been forward thinking in the education of ladies, and as such was the social inferior of the rest of the ladies. Even Miss Appleby boasted an impoverished baronet somewhere in her family tree, but Miss Micklethwaite had no such claims to gentility. She was far too proud "to ape her betters" as she declared when referring to her brother's wife whose father had made a fortune in trade. Therefore the ladies settled on some dark sturdy poplin (which had served as a voluminous coat to protect her mother's extraordinary gowns) which could form a simple habit and some black figured muslin that could be fashioned into a simple evening gown. They had such an abundance of beautiful furs in ermine and sable that they almost decided to trim a hat and muff for her, but it would not do - she would not have worn it. It was only when Clarissa found a fox stole at the very bottom of the trunk, which could very well do the same purpose, that she was satisfied.

'For she cannot object to that,' declared Clarissa stoutly, 'since it is such as anyone with a respectable allowance might possess.'

The ladies took such of their spoils as they wished to their sitting room, there to begin cutting and pinning to their hearts' delight. They were found so by Misses Micklethwaite and Appleby, returned from their constitutional. When they were informed what was toward, Miss Appleby began to cry, 'Oh my dear girl, you cannot. I have never had such gowns in my life ... your dear mama ...'

'Would be happy to see you wear them and glad that you could add a little to my consequence with my new neighbours. It would not do, you know, for them to think me a nip-cheese to my companion. And you need not think me generous, you know, for they will cost me nothing *and* you will be obliged to help make them.'

'Oh, of course ...' said Miss Appleby, still sobbing with gratitude.

'Stop snivelling and give the girls a hand, Louisa. It is quite right, you cannot show Clarissa up with her neighbours - even I can see that. Give me the poplin, I'll see to it. If you think that you two girls will measure me then you are much mistaken. A fox-trimmed bonnet. Whatever next. I'll be as fine as my fool of a sister-in-law,' she added with grim humour. It seemed to Clarissa that her sister-in-law had been spared much by their departure to Hertfordshire.

In the next few days the ladies trimmed bonnets made a number of simple dresses (with the help of a girl from the village), all of which were given a little 'town gloss' by the eagle eye of Miss Petersham (so lately one of the town's leading beauties) and packed the more colourful treasures for use at a later date. They also had to hire a postchaise (and four, for Clarissa had decided to arrive in style) and had calculated that the journey could be done with only one night at an inn. The small sum that had been left to her by her mother was dwindling fast (a fact she must keep from her companions) and she knew that it might last her some six months only in the country. Oriana thought that they should strive to give a respectable front: any show of poverty might lead unscrupulous persons to believe them open to swindle. They wrote letters to their various relatives telling them of their plans in the vaguest terms possible. Clarissa knew that hers would cross her brother on the road but she wished to be able to say that she had sent it. Really, she was becoming quite duplicitous.

Miss Petersham possessed some fine simple gowns which she had brought from her home, but she directed a missive to her brother's butler direct to send on her trunks to Hertfordshire. It would be seen as a pretty poor show if he forbade this - which Oriana knew he would wish to do. He could have ignored such a request if it was directed at *him,* but she hardly thought he would care to display his ill-temper to Settings, the butler without whom life at home would cease to run smoothly. Oriana felt herself to be duplicitous too, but she was far less repentant than Clarissa.

All of them were imbued with new energy and vigour, for they saw that they had had a close escape from becoming the despised poor relations, and could look forward to an adventure that might be fraught with challenge, but in which they might really be *useful.*

When Miss Appleby had shared her misgivings to Miss Micklethwaite about the wisdom of their enterprise and her hope that she would not be a burden to her dear Clarissa, her friend was as forthright as always.

'I understand your feelings, Louisa, but think a little. If this all comes to naught then we will all just go back to our original plan. You and I to drudge for our family,' here Miss Appleby gave an obligatory sound of protest, ignored by her friend, 'Oriana to be under the will of her brute of a brother, and Clarissa to sell the estate and return home to that prosy bore she's related to. However, if it does take off, we should have been real use to her. She could not well manage so ambitious a plan without us. I can knock the house into shape if it's not too far gone. You can keep up with the genteel side of things, that ladylike way of behaving in company that I was not brought up to nor, since she has been brought up here, has Clarissa. Oriana can help with the estate but Clarissa and she are far too pretty to be able to keep the pack of hounds that will be paying them calls if I'm not mistaken. They shall need us to give them countenance.'

'Indeed, my dear Augusta, we *must* go!' said Miss Appleby

Though it seemed impossible to believe, they found themselves tucked up in a neat postchaise, resplendent in their newly trimmed pelisses and bonnets, setting off to Hertfordshire fully three days before Mr Thorne was due to arrive. Since it clearly would not do to travel on Sunday, they sat off in fine fettle early on Friday morning, with the early spring frosts nipping at the air, full of hope for the new life ahead of them and some sad thoughts for the life they had left behind. Clarissa looked at the sparkle in her friends' eyes, and was satisfied.

CHAPTER 3

A Brother Thwarted

Cornelia Thorne had, until recently, no desire to house her husband's orphaned sister, her house having only three guest bedrooms. She had made representations to her husband on this head but he had felt that his father would have expected no less of him. When Cornelia thought that Clarissa would not mind one of the attic rooms, to be nearer to the darling children, it did not cross her mind that her own bedchamber was as far away from her children's as it was reasonably possible to be. At first, John had no fault to find with this scheme, but upon reflection he thought it might not be thought well of in the village of Little Sowersby if it became known. When his sister, father and stepmother had visited him last, Clarissa had made friends in the village, including Juliana Sowersby, the daughter of the manor. It would not do, he explained to his wife, to be thought shabby by the Sowersbys.

Though Cornelia complained of her house to all that knew her as cramped, it was larger indeed than in her parents' home in Warwickshire. Mrs Thorne had taken a step up in the world in marrying John, her solid husband whose small independence allowed them to keep their home in a genteel manner, but forbade the luxuries that her heart craved. She kept a cook-maid, a groom, and of course a nurse for her three energetic children, but she decried to her special friends the lack of a lady's maid. Many felt sorry for the tumble that Cornelia was thought to have taken in life, but many more saw through her and simply thought she gave herself airs.

She was a pretty woman, with an abundance of brown hair which she kept dressed in the latest mode, and a rounded figure hardly affected by child bearing. Her husband could perceive no fault in her, she was petted and indulged by him in every way, but since neither of them could bear to be less than respectable this did not lead them towards debt. In the sudden inheritance of a large estate by his sister (why was *her* mother so much better connected that John's, in every other way the superior woman?) Cornelia saw a way of introducing much more money into her household with her arrival.

So it was that as she was packing her husband's portmanteau for his journey she was charging him to deliver sweet messages to Clarissa.

'Do tell my dearest sister that I shall be in transports to see her again. As will William and Percy and little Bella be to see their dear aunt.'

Though he doubted that the children would remember their 'dear aunt', John took this speech in the spirit it was meant. 'You are all generosity, my dear, to one whose pert manners might have given you disgust.' He regarded his wife with a tenderness that was seen rarely in his eyes. He regarded the world through suspicious eyes, set into a grave face. Inclined to early portliness and not a little pomposity, he looked a good deal older than his thirty years.

Completely forgetting what she had called Clarissa after her last visit, Cornelia smiled in a saintly way. 'Well, I trust that I would never criticize your late step-mama, but let us just say that Clarissa will no doubt benefit from the *tone* of a well-ordered household and the moral guidance of her older brother.'

Since Clarissa had seldom shown any tendency to follow his moral lead, John might have doubted this. However, his wife's glowing opinion of him allowed him to ignore this and set off in good heart to bring his sister back to her new home.

In the inside pocket of his greatcoat were certain papers that his lawyer had drawn up for him, wanting only Clarissa's signature to allow him to sell the estate and bank any other incomes accrued. His lawyer agreed with him that the funds and income had best be handled by themselves, allowing of course the young lady an income of, say, one hundred pounds a quarter. This, John had not been inclined to permit, since it gave Clarissa an income for fripperies, which quite outdid his wife's. The lawyer had been all understanding - it would quite unbalance the household. A much smaller allowance then, with monies due put into the housekeeping, and the large funds invested and a small commission taken by her brother for increasing her profits. His wife agreed with him - for what could a young lady know of business? It would be relief to Clarissa for John to take it out of her hands.

When she signed the papers, Clarissa may never trouble her head with such things again. John rode on his way portentously, thinking of the investments that his man of business recommended, for it never occurred to the young man that any female, even one as unnatural as his sister, could fail to see the advantages to his scheme. He knew himself to be a dutiful brother, and was proud.

He arrived at the academy as Mr Peterkin (who had come to try his luck with Clarissa again) was coming away from the door in great agitation of spirit.

'Sir,' he exclaimed, 'Mr Thorne. Can it be that you have come to visit your unhappy sister.'

'Do I know you, sir?' uttered Mr Thorne, removing from his arm Mr Peterkin's clutching fingers.

'Indeed - upon your last visit - my name is Hubert Peterkin - the Reverend Mr Norbert's curate, you know. Can it be that you do not know that your sister has gone?'

'Nonsense,' declared Mr Thorne and continued on his way to the door confidently. As he approached, he felt that confidence ebb away as he saw all the unmistakable signs of a house that had been closed up.

Peterkin ran after him, talking all the time. 'This is most ill-conceived, you must agree sir, but indeed it is true. Your sister had departed to Hertfordshire, as her cook, Jane, has just informed me. There is no use in looking for the knocker, sir. It has been removed. I had myself to go around to the kitchens to get an answer. Jane is merely waiting for the agent to arrive this day, sir.'

'Hertfordshire,' declared Thorne, 'Can she have gone to Ashcroft alone?'

'As to that, sir, I believe *all* the ladies have gone. But I do think they should have informed me. *I*, of all people, have a right to know.'

Petersham looked at the balding curate with his face purple from the exertion of following his long strides with outraged bewilderment. '*You,* sir? *You* have the right to know my sister's business. How is this so?'

The curate was aware of having been betrayed by his anxiety into saying too much. 'Well sir ... that is ... I have had the honour of asking your sister to be my wife. Left alone in the world as she was, I felt it my duty to...' He came to a halt under the affronted gaze of Mr Thorne.

'My sister, sir, is not alone in the world,' he said in frigid accents, 'and even if she was, I doubt that she would have accepted an offer from one as distant to her as you.' His raking glance seemed to take in the frayed shirt cuff that Peterkin was hiding up his sleeve and the grease spot that Molly had been unable to remove from his hat. He shrank, uttering a protest about a clergyman's position being as high as any in the land but hardly loud enough for the stiff young man to hear him before he had marched past and enjoined his coachman to take him to the nearest inn.

'I would advise you sir, not to speak of my sister's business abroad, for it can be no concern of yours.' Then he bethought himself of another matter.

'What did you mean *all* the ladies?'

Mr Peterkin recovered and in a failing voice told him who had accompanied his sister.

As Thorne drove away he was both incensed and relieved at this news. It was just like Clarissa to take on a parcel of poor relations but at least she was sensible enough not to damage her reputation by racketing about the countryside unattended. Though he could ill afford the extra expense, he was tempted to post onwards to Ashcroft and call a halt to whatever foolish and ungrateful scheme Clarissa was hatching. Over a warm nuncheon at a cosy inn, he considered further.

Upon reflection, he thought that the papers in his pocket were unlikely to be signed by a young lady at outs with her brother. He did not doubt his will over hers in the long-term, but he wished to expedite matters.

The state of Ashcroft, the neglect of the house and grounds, and the general disorder of the estate would not be the home that Clarissa and her four companions might hope for. Even *he* did not have the expertise needed to revive such a big estate, so he almost laughed when he thought of what Clarissa's feelings might be. His man of business had advised him that making the estate profitable would cost a great deal of time and money; and when he had visited it he had believed him. Much better to sell it to one of the newly rich merchants, with a *penchant* for an historic house in the country and with the wealth to do something with it, or to Lord Staines from a neighbouring estate who had declared a flattering interest when he had been in Hertfordshire.

He would drive home and hope that by allowing Clarissa a month in that miserable place she would see what she was up against and return home with her brother a chastened young lady, ready to sign the papers. He trusted that the ladies would find, on their travels, that they were very unwise to have set out without a man to guide them.

Had he but known it, the posting inn at which they had stopped for the night had offered them a small adventure - one that might not have occurred if he had accompanied them.

Its taproom had been occupied by a crowd of young gentlemen who had no doubt come to witness some sporting event in the area but now had nothing better to do than drink the landlord's excellent brandy and gin. Miss Micklethwaite took in the situation at a glance and made sure to stand guard at the door whilst the rest of the party were ushered upstairs by the landlady. She was perceived to be an honest countrywoman who appeared honoured by the ladies' visit and bobbed so many curtsies to them that Clarissa laughed under her breath and whispered to Miss Petersham, 'See what attentions a sable muff will bring you.'

Oriana was reminded that she had left her muff in the carriage and broke away from the others to retrieve it. As she came back, one of the young bucks that had just left the taproom set eyes on her and exclaimed, 'Miss Petersham.' The gentleman in the shadows behind him raised his head quickly, as did the redoubtable Miss Micklethwaite.

Oriana was so startled that she dropped her reticule. Her voice had its icy cool, however, when she replied, 'Mr Booth. How strange to encounter you,' as she recognized a young admirer from her London season.

Mr Booth was about twenty-four years old and his eyes were red and glittering from the spirits that he had imbibed, 'How strange, ma'am, for me to encounter an *angel*,' he countered, with a distinct slur in his voice. He proceeded to remove his hat and sweep a magnificent bow before her, quite barring her way from entering the inn. It seemed that the other, older gentleman must have moved forward but before he did, Miss Micklethwaite swept forward knocking the young man's hat into the mud (perhaps accidentally) and desiring him to stop making a cake of himself. 'Goodnight to you, sir,' she said, drawing Oriana forward, 'and if you were a gentleman you would know better than to go about addressing young ladies in common inn-yards.'

'But ... I am acquainted with this young lady ...' protested Mr Booth in vain, for the ladies had entered the inn.

'Alas, Charles, you should not address young ladies - even if acquainted with them - when you are three parts drunk.'

Mr Booth turned to look at the gentleman who had thus addressed him. He was a man in his early thirties, his height of over six foot enough to draw attention as did the elegance of his attire, even in his topboots and buckskins, making it evident he was both wealthy and fashionable. His face was not handsome, but dark and saturnine, giving him a dangerous look that both thrilled and terrified many ladies of his acquaintance.

'Grandiston. Did you see who that was? Miss Petersham. I thought her brother had said she was abroad with some relatives after the scandal when she cried off from old Charteris.'

'No doubt he did. If her brother is not given to dissembling we must assume that she has but lately returned. But I fear for his immortal soul,' he said smoothly, returning Mr Booth's hat to him. His tone was light and honeyed, but always there was a hint of menace in his tone when he spoke like this.

'Why do you say so?' said Booth, and turned to re-enter the taproom.

'In a moment, my boy, in a moment,' he strode off abruptly and had a brief conversation with a post-boy in the yard. Booth saw coin change hands as the Earl of Grandiston returned with a satisfied smile on his face. 'Well, well,' he said, 'look what chance flings my way.' He put his arms on the young man's shoulder and drew him into the taproom. 'But you wished to know why I doubt her brother - merely knowledge of his character. It *may* have been true but it may not. As a young cub he was wont to say whatever would best serve him. Most unlike his father or sister whose bluntness, as I have cause to know, was not always in accordance with modern manners ...' Grandiston paused and smiled as though at some wicked reminiscence, '... but refreshing all the same.'

'You were a friend of Petersham's, were you not, before you went off to the Peninsular?'

'I was, my young sot, but have another drink and strive not to start another conversation about my military career - you know I find it a dead bore.'

As his young friend did as he bade him, Grandiston lounged on the wooden settle of the taproom playing negligently with his quizzing-glass looking very much the sporting gentleman.

He was aware that his one-time intended bride was preparing to retire in the bedroom above him but he doubted that she knew of her father's plans. When his dearest friend, Sir Ralph Petersham, had confided his desire to betroth his daughter to him, he had looked at the sixteen-year-old beauty with astonishment.

As he observed her progress in the next two years as she tumbled off of her high spirited hunters, her imperious manner to all who would thwart her will, her gentle manner to her servants or social inferiors and her love of the estate and all its tenants, he felt that she was just the wife that he had always dreamed of.

They had fought and laughed together as they rode the farmlands, but only once had anything more than a sisterly feeling shown in her. It was when the rumour reached her, from a friend who had had her come-out in London the season before Oriana's, of his flirtation, and supposed intentions towards a certain Miss Hazlehurst.

Oriana had tried to draw him out on the matter and when he had chosen to quiz her for her interest, she had flown at him angrily, saying she could not imagine any lady willing to marry a man as ugly as the devil himself. With others, Miss Petersham was the ice queen, but with him a raging virago.

Her jealousy had raised his passions - but the war intervened. He could not look at events in Europe and do nothing. He could not speak to Miss Petersham while his future was uncertain. He accepted a commission and had spent the past two years in the mud of Portugal with the valiant forces of Wellington. Unfortunately, he found himself so frequently digging balls out of his body that Wellington himself sent him home. 'For God's sake man, a man's system can only take so much. You've done your bit for war. I only wish I had.'

Oriana had never known his intentions but when he heard of her father's death and her engagement to Charteris he felt that she had somehow betrayed him and herself by taking a rich husband. He was in England again before he knew of the scandal of the broken engagement and when he had applied at her home to find her he had met with the squirming equivocations of her brother. He had seen at a glance that young Petersham had behaved in some scoundrel fashion to his sister and it was only his breeding that had prevented him wringing out of him Oriana's direction. Not whilst a guest in his house, but Grandiston had not yet finished with Fitzroy Petersham. Now barely two weeks later, Oriana Petersham lay upstairs in her bed, more beautiful and desirable than ever. He knew where she was bound, and like the general that his friends in the regiment had called him, he slowly considered his strategy in this next campaign.

CHAPTER 4

The Word Spreads

Sir Fitzroy Petersham received his sister's letter with annoyance. He had tried to forget her existence in the year since her dreadful disobedience and the short-lived scandal of the broken engagement. That there would never have been a scandal had he not put the announcement of the marriage into the *Morning Post* without first consulting the prospective bride, he did not consider at all. As usual his sister, favourite of his late father and mother, had humiliated him. Oriana's dashed popularity in her London season had meant that much of her acquaintance had continued to inquire after her and he had been obliged to prevaricate as to her whereabouts, passing it off as a visit to friends abroad. He could not well say that his sister would rather teach in a girls' school than live with him and he worried that the daughter of one of his friends might one day be taught by his sister. However, most members of the *ton* had ignored the school which promised to educate young ladies in Latin and Greek and other subjects unnecessary, indeed, undesirable, for fashionable young ladies. He had suffered the visit from Grandiston and now he had to worry what next she would do. Would his friends accept a story of Oriana lending her companionship to a friend? Perhaps this might actually take the pressure off him; he could furnish her friends with her new direction.

He was a handsome young man of athletic build like his father, but without any strength of character on his dark good looks. He had been pleased to accede to his father's dignities at the age of twenty-three, but apart from spending a great deal of money he had changed very little. He had taken to ordering the servants with all of his father's imperiousness, but without his fairness, and knew himself to be despised by them. He fancied himself to be a sporting gentleman, but he was too craven in the saddle to attempt the heroics of his father or sister. His mother had indulged his sulks and he missed her greatly. He had many acquaintances, but no close friends, and he would have welcomed Oriana's presence in his great empty house, if only so that he could bully her and allow her to run the estate as she always had. He was tired of his agent asking him to make decisions about his dashed tenants. Her contempt, however, he could not have borne. The servants, at least, could not display theirs'.

He had determined to go to London, but hoped to avoid another uncomfortable conversation with Grandiston. What concern of *his* was Oriana's welfare? He behaved as though she had been consigned to his care. It was for her brother to decide upon her future. Yet again, Oriana had pre-empted his control of her and he did not like it but he could not well decide upon the right course of action.

As chance would have it, he was accosted in Albemarle Street by the Honourable Charles Booth, nattily attired in blue long-tailed coat and a yellow waistcoat.

'Ah, Petersham.'

'Booth. I thought you would be out of town at this season.' Petersham had not given it any thought at all, for Booth was not one of his intimates and he was a trifle surprised to be hailed by him.

'Visiting my mother. She's been kept in town by an outbreak of measles in the younger sprogs. Met your sister on the road, the other day. She was looking in great beauty,' said Booth easily. He was obliged to suppress a wider grin as he saw Petersham stiffen. Grandiston was always right. He'd said that the baronet would squirm at the mention of his sister. What mystery lay here?

'Yes, indeed,' was the reply, 'she is bearing an ... an old school friend company for some time. Viscount Ashcroft's heiress, you know.' Petersham was uneasily aware that he had just committed himself to accepting Oriana's newest start in the eyes of the polite world.

Young Booth was a sporting gentleman and now he scented fear in his quarry even though he did not understand its cause. 'Thought your sister was educated at home. Well I know she was, for your mamma passed on the governess to my sisters.'

'Of course she was,' said Sir Fitzroy testily, 'I only meant that she met Miss Thorne when *she* was at school. I have an appointment, Booth, so I'll bid you good-day.'

Booth doffed his hat. 'Certainly, old boy. Misunderstanding - so sorry.' He permitted himself a grin as he gaily bowled up the street towards his club, twirling his cane and rehearsing an account of this meeting to recount to Grandiston who was presently ensconced there. His lively brain (when not befuddled with foul spirits) began to consider. Could they be going to Ashcroft? Surely not, for poor old Bosky (Viscount Ashcroft, to the uninitiated) had let it go to rack and ruin before his premature but unsurprising death.

He asked this question of Grandiston ten minutes later.

'Well deduced, my boy. I believe that is just where they were going,' said his friend smoothly.

'I shouldn't have thought that it was any place fit for ladies. There's hardly been time to put it to rights since Bosky's death and the last time I was there ...'

'Yes, yes light-skirts riding the backs of young bucks in betting races, champagne in washing ewers and every kind of dissipation imaginable. I've heard the scandal,' interrupted Grandiston. He cocked an eyebrow at his young companion. 'What I didn't know, though, was that you were a member of that set, Charles.'

'I was not,' flashed Booth, 'Oh, you're joking Grandiston. I might have known. I went up there to collect a hunter that Ashcroft was selling. I never saw such a rum lot in my life. *They* may have fancied that they were enjoying themselves but it looked ludicrous to me. The doxies that they employed were a sure way to get the pox. I take my pleasure in safer places.'

'Your friends must welcome the wisdom if not the morality of that last remark. It is time, my lad, that you got married and adopted a life of rectitude.'

Booth laughed but was not diverted. 'If her suitors knew that she was at Ashcroft, I daresay that they would be posting to Hertfordshire in droves.'

'I daresay,' drawled Grandiston at his most dry, 'but I trust, dear Charles, that the town may not know her whereabouts for some time.' The message was unmistakable.

'Oh, certainly, my dear sir,' said Booth blithely, 'you can depend upon me.'

'I'll let you know, Charles, when I wish the world to know,' said Grandiston, his dark eyes glittering, 'Then I'll depend on you to spread the word.'

Booth was too much in awe of his older friend to question him too closely but he remarked. 'I believe that Hertfordshire is pleasant at this time of year. I think Staines has a house there.'

'Ahead of the pack, Charles, that's the spirit.' He poured another glass of wine. 'Perhaps we should honour his Lordship with a visit.'

Lord Ferdinand Staines became aware of the imminent arrival of the new tenant at Ashcroft from an unimpeachable source, his mother. This lady was reclining on a lilac chaise, wearing a clashing orange robe over pale green gauze nightdress and a lace cap fastened over her suspiciously blonde curls. When her son entered, she went so far as to sit up and say, 'Do you know that that girl is coming to Ashcroft?'

His Lordship could never see his mother's attire without it being a shock to his superior taste, but he had learned that there was no point in giving her a hint. Just as well, he thought, that her stubbornness had been passed on to him as manly firmness. 'Well, I suppose her brother must bring her to see for herself what a shocking state it's in, *if* you mean Miss Thorne, as I presume you do. There is no need to get in a curl, Mamma, I doubt that she will be in the neighbourhood long enough to see her. The brother and I have it quite decided between us.'

His mother eyed her son with annoyance. Even on quite handsome men like her tall blonde son, his hair brushed into the fashionable Brutus, his boots with their mirror shine, that air of self-satisfied certainty was unattractive. Still less when directed at one who had dandled him on her knee. 'Well, you are quite out there. She has sent a servant ahead of her and he has been putting the place to rights for her arrival. He sent off that London butler who was there, packing – caught him stealing in the cellar, I believe – and sent some village girls to clean. Obviously it is to be an extended visit.'

'I can hardly believe it. How can you know this?'

She was glad to see the complacent look wiped from his face but she sighed. Men never had the least idea how things work in the country if it isn't hunting or farming, or such like. 'Well as it happens, Sullivan, the girl's butler, is a local boy, related distantly to our groom. He was first footman in the *old* viscount's time and left Ashcroft with Lady Clara when she made that ridiculous marriage to that philosopher, or whatever he was. Devoted to her, they say, but *our* Sullivan says the old viscount still paid his salary to look after his daughter. Well, whatever that may be, he's back and preparing the ground for that chit of a girl. Her mother was a foolish, forward creature far, *far* too indulged by her father. He never could stand his son, you know, and that may very well have ruined him. Your father would have it that he wasn't a true Ashcroft at all, but for my money that was all talk - old Lady Ashcroft wouldn't have behaved in that way until she had an heir *at least*. Mind you, the late viscount didn't at all resemble his father, but ...' she broke off as her son gave an impatient sigh, 'but I don't suppose,' she said with dignity, 'that you wish to hear about that. What do you propose to do about Ashcroft?'

Her son's air of complacency returned and he sat down and crossed his legs, '*First,* I shall wait to see if all this servants' gossip has any basis in *fact* Mamma,' he said it as if 'fact' were a word she was not acquainted with. '*If* so, I shall give the girl time to see how ridiculous it is for her to contemplate residing at Ashcroft, which I shall carefully explain to her when first I set eyes upon her.' With this he snapped his newspaper in front of him and began perusing it.

It is to be hoped, thought his fond mamma, that Miss Thorne would not greet his careful explanations with the same simmering resentment that they produced in her.

Unaware of the machinations of members of the polite world, the ladies were wearily reaching the end of their journey. As they entered the park, Miss Appleby leaned out of the coach and said, 'Look, there. What a handsome house, though thankfully not as large as I thought. She pointed to a square building with Roman columns at the front whose windows, at the front, she counted as eight.

'Well, I was a child when I was last here, but I *believe* that is the Dower House,' said Clarissa.

'Good gracious.' shrieked Miss Appleby, faintly.

They could not well see the grounds but a quarter of a mile further up the drive, the large and looming shape of Ashcroft Manor appeared.

'Well,' said Miss Micklethwaite. 'Impressive indeed.'

Though the moon was full and caught the windows in her gaze, Miss Appleby lost count of them.

The door was opened and on the steps stood the redoubtable Sullivan.

'I fancy you could do with some supper, ladies. It is served in the front saloon.'

The ladies walked into a hall that took their respective breaths away. A grand oak staircase swept up to the floors above from an Italian marble floor whose acreage astounded them. It was, however, excessively draughty, so the ladies moved quickly towards the flickering candles and roaring fire, which could be seen beyond some doors that opened on to the hall. There some tea and a variety of warm dishes met their eyes and they went in gladly to refresh themselves. Sullivan be blessed.

Clarissa, however, had only partaken of a cup of tea and a pastry when she declared her intention to view the house. She begged her companions to make a hearty supper however, and took up a candlestick to go unaccompanied but for Sullivan. She gave him some grateful words and then set off around the house, lately the seat of a viscount and now unaccountably owned by an eighteen-year-old girl, scarcely out of the schoolroom.

When she re-joined the ladies she was in a better heart than was expected.

'Well, there is a great deal of old fashioned furniture cluttering many of the rooms but I think you will be heartened at your accommodations tonight ladies. Such luxury. Sullivan has lit a fire in each bedchamber and placed hot bricks for our feet. The rest of the house is in a good state barring the West Wing which Sullivan says is riddled with damp and many other evils and should be shut up for the present. Still I feel we can manage with the remaining six public rooms and fourteen bedrooms. The linen closets are completely neglected, of course, but we may soon see to that. Apart from cleaning, sorting the best furniture into the rooms that we choose to use and having the chimneys swept I daresay we shall have nothing to do, shall we, Sullivan?' she said merrily.

Sullivan allowed his long, lugubrious face a brief smile, 'As to that Miss Clarissa, I have yet to discuss the kitchen range - most uncooperative it is being. The only one who could manage it was Mrs Stebbings, the cook in the old master's time. Then there's the estate itself, miss. It quite breaks my heart to see it as it is now. The gardens need a proper overhaul miss, and the state of the tenants' cottages –well, Miss Clarissa, I'm glad your poor mamma is not here to see it, for it would have broken her and no mistake.'

'Well,' said Miss Micklethwaite, noticing that Clarissa's brave smile was failing under this depressing list, 'There's no call to scare us to death on our first night, Sullivan. Miss Clarissa will give orders in the morning.'

'Yes, ma'am. I beg your pardon. Might I just say, Mr Elfoy the agent for the estate begged leave to visit you tomorrow, Miss Clarissa? He said it was urgent, ma'am, but I will deny you if you wish.'

Clarissa, who was looking a trifle worn out by the dawning of her new responsibilities, said, 'No Sullivan, quite right. We must begin as soon as is possible.' Quite suddenly overcome, she began to cry.

Sullivan drew tactfully from the room, cursing himself silently for failing to perceive how overwhelming this house must be for such a very young lady and resolving to be careful in future.

'Take her to bed, Louisa. She's knocked out and it is not to be wondered at,' said the eldest of the ladies.

'Indeed I'm all right, Waity, I cannot imagine ...,' said Clarissa; the tears coursing down her cheeks.

'No indeed, dear,' cooed Miss Appleby, drawing her forward and putting her arm around her waist. 'Nothing that a little sleep won't cure. Come with me, now dear.' And she drew her up towards the stairs.

Miss Petersham turned to her companion, 'Oh, Waity, it is easy to forget that Clarissa is such a young girl. Losing her mamma so soon after her father's death - it's no wonder that this now should overwhelm her. She is such a redoubtable girl that she will no doubt seem fine in the morning but we must watch her carefully.'

'Indeed,' said Miss Micklethwaite, 'She will feel better when we start to *do* something. Do you know, apart from not being able to face life with her prosy brother and his cooing little wife, I think it's the doing that Clarissa craves. She *needs* this place so that she does not dwell on those subjects that depress her spirits. In that she's her mother's daughter. She'll come about.'

'Yes, all of us need that,' Oriana took a turn about the room. 'We're freaks you know, Waity.All of us, except poor Appleby, perhaps. We are freaks of nature who would dare question the will of the men whose position it is to guide us. Some women would have taken the curate's offer, or at least waited until a better one arrived; but the cast of our minds being as they are we can allow no man to rule without respect. At least here we should be free of those who would blight us with their attentions.'

'Well, as to that my dear, I have seldom been blighted by a man's attentions,' said Miss Micklethwaite mildly, 'but I am glad, in theory, to be free of it.' Oriana smiled at this, but still looked tired. Her friend drew her from the room gently. 'Time for bed before you work yourself into just such a state as Clarissa.'

Chapter 5

The Ladies at Home

Clarissa awoke the next morning to the sight of a slight young girl wearing a cap, brown dress and apron pulling open the window drapes and letting the early sunlight seep over her counterpane.

'But who are you?' said Clarissa sitting up.

'Why, your lady's maid Becky, if it pleases you, miss,' she replied and bustled forward with a shawl for Clarissa's shoulders and placed a cup of chocolate into her hands. 'Mr Sullivan employed me from the village, miss, seeing as how you had to leave your maid behind. I've not all the experience that you might like miss - this is a step up for me, you might say - but I can dress hair and I'm clever with a needle.' Becky's round face looked a trifle anxiously at Clarissa.

'I'm sure of that,' said Clarissa, 'Thank you Becky, you can go now, I'll dress myself this morning.' Becky looked disappointed, but bobbed a curtsy and departed.

As she settled back on the bank of feather pillows sipping her chocolate, Clarissa thought that she had never known such luxury. Her bed was big enough for a cavalry regiment to sleep in and was moreover hung with straw-coloured silk. Her room was enormous, so it seemed to her, and was appointed with elegant furniture. She guessed this to have been her aunt's room, and her silver-backed brush set still adorned the dressing table with its exquisite French mirror. That the maid was an elegance Sullivan had required to add to her consequence in the neighbourhood was something she did not doubt; but it was a welcome luxury. Well it was time to start her day as lady of the manor. Almost at variance with this thought was that she put on her oldest grey dress.

The ladies cried out at her appearance, but Clarissa only said 'There's a great deal of work to be done and I don't mean to spoil my dresses.'

And so it was that as she was unpacking their cherished books in the library, Mr Elfoy found her.

That gentleman had come to the house, but on passing the library windows on route to the front doors, he had heard a shriek and entered. He found a young girl in a shabby grey gown and apron holding her toe and hopping about the room. She heard him laugh and looked around.

She saw a young man of devastating attractiveness. He was tall and of athletic build and his rich chestnut hair, though severely brushed from his noble forehead, was a riot of curls, one having escaped across his brow in a way that drew attention to his laughing eyes. These were of a velvet autumnal colour, with lashes that would be the envy of most young ladies. The draw of his eyes was such that Clarissa hardly noticed his firm jaw-line or his rakishly dimpled chin. He was dressed with quiet propriety in a blue coat, but however provincial his tailor, his magnificent form could not but make it look like a masterpiece.

Her face turned towards him and quite naturally returned his grin. Despite the smut on her face Mr Elfoy warmed to her, 'Hello there, have you hurt yourself? My name's Elfoy and I've come to see your mistress.'

Clarissa was stunned – what a figure she must cut. So she said, 'Yes sir. I'll find her.' and disappeared quickly. She met Miss Micklethwaite and Oriana in the hallway as she came running in disorder from the library.

'Oh, Waity, Mr Elfoy the agent is in the library. Pray bear him company and tell him I'll be along in some minutes. Oriana!' cried Clarissa, grasping her hands, 'Can you do *something* with my hair? Please come up with me.'

Casting a bewildered glance at Miss Micklethwaite, Oriana murmured, 'Of course, my dear.'

It was a very different Clarissa who presented herself to Mr Elfoy presently. Miss Micklethwaite gave a start on seeing her, for never had Clarissa given so much attention to her appearance. How Clarissa's hair came to be cut at the front and coaxed into clustering curls that framed her face so becomingly and then swept into a Grecian arrangement with black satin ribbons in a scant half-hour was beyond her. She was now more correctly attired in her new black muslin, high at the neck and trimmed with the Brussels' lace from her mamma's chest. Her eye had a sparkle about it that Miss Micklethwaite had never seen as she held out her hand in welcome to Mr Elfoy.

'Ah, here is Miss Thorne now,' she said stoutly.

The handsome, easy-mannered young man that she had been conversing with for the half-hour previously had seemed to become turned to stone. Then a flush rose on his cheek and he became animated enough to clasp the hand that was being held out to him. That this was the same young woman whom he had supposed a maid, he had no doubt. He did not exactly see how it had been achieved but that he was dealing with a young lady of the first quality was quite obvious. How had he come to make such a mistake? Her chin was regally held, he felt a fool of the first order. He began a tangled apology.

'Miss Thorne. How rude you must have thought me. I did not know, I could not have guessed ...' he stopped, realising he was getting himself into deeper water.

Clarissa took pity on him.

'Well of course not, sir, such a figure I must have cut in my old work gown. Don't give it another thought,' and she smiled her smile of this afternoon in the friendliest manner, gesturing to take his seat. As she sat down her eyes teased him, 'Now we have both been a little embarrassed, haven't we?'

Mr Elfoy found himself grinning again, causing her to dimple merrily. Good goodness, he thought, I am undone. How perfect she is and how I know I must not think such things about my employer.

Oriana noted with amusement that her entrance had passed the young man by. Although not a conceited girl, she was nevertheless used to drawing male eyes – and what superior eyes Mr Elfoy possessed. And was it possible that Clarissa was flirting? The burns from the hot iron still smarted on Oriana's hands, for Clarissa had urged her maid and Oriana to make haste upstairs and twisted and turned whilst it was being done. When finally it was finished she had looked into the mirror appreciatively. 'Now at least I shall not be taken for a servant.'

Oriana had replied, 'No, indeed.'

She now exchanged amused glances with Miss Mickleth-waite who was still reeling at the change in Clarissa. One glance at the handsome young agent was quite enough to explain her friend's behaviour.

Clarissa and he discussed the estate, with Oriana called to participate, asking questions that Mr Elfoy saw at once to be apposite and full of knowledge that he had not believed young ladies to possess. Indeed he was stunned by how much of what was said that Clarissa grasped and he was hopeful that, at last, a good landlord might put the estate to rights.

'The truth is, Mr Elfoy, that all of what you say needs done must be done from what revenues we now have. I bring no money to help with any of this,' said Clarissa with her usual candour, 'Perhaps you believe it cannot be done?'

Mr Elfoy blushed again, to his own irritation. 'There may be some help with this, Miss Thorne, but we must act fast. Of course, it will not cover all the repairs and improvements, but ...'

Oriana laughed, 'For goodness sake, sir, we are all agog. What is it?'

'The Dower House: it has been well looked after by an aunt of the previous viscount and is now vacant. If you would not object to a tenant, Ma'am, I believe that the rent might allow us to begin. The last viscount would not have tenants since he liked to have his, well, his privacy ...'

'Don't be mealy-mouthed, young man,' interrupted Miss Micklethwaite, 'we all know what a libertine the late viscount was. We can imagine that he did not want his – pleasures - to be overlooked by the world.'

'Indeed, yes,' said Clarissa, 'my late cousin seems to have been a strange person - but never mind that. Let it be a tenant sir, and as soon as maybe. We shall leave the matter entirely in your hands. Do call tomorrow and ride with Miss Petersham and myself around the estate, I shall be most obliged if you could introduce me to the tenant farmers.'

As Mr Elfoy left with a singing heart, Clarissa began to be teased by her companions. She did not attend, however. She had thought that she had just wanted to play a trick on Mr Elfoy, but she discovered that his obvious admiration had had an effect on her as did his easy grin and his sense of the ridiculous. Never had she felt so - so *elevated* in the presence of a young man. She knew, however, that it would be wrong to think of him. Their situations were very different. Though as a gentleman's son of small means he might have been a proper suitor for her six months ago, he would no longer feel himself equal to court the lady of the manor. It was unfortunate, but her mind was too full of the tasks ahead to feel much pain.

Chapter 6

Settling In

In the days that followed, a pattern developed. Clarissa and Oriana rode on the estate with Mr Elfoy, meeting her tenants, and Miss Micklethwaite and Miss Appleby set to on the linen and the hot houses making energetic use of their time. The girls that had been employed to help had never worked so hard and soon order began to be established and portions of the house polished and shone as it had in its glory days. They banished tired and damaged furniture to the attics and discovered beautiful pieces in the plethora of upstairs rooms to replace them.

When Clarissa evinced a desire for the grounds (at least those immediately around the house) to be put to rights, Mr Elfoy led her to meet Muggins, a tenant farmer on the estate whose father had directed the regiment of gardeners in her uncle's time.

Oriana, a little behind Clarissa and Mr Elfoy, saw a strong square man with a look of defiance on his face and wondered if trouble might not come. He was a broad, fiercely strong man in his twenties, wearing a striped shirt that was frayed but had been put on clean this morning. The yard had a well-kept look to it and Oriana deduced a good tenant. So what was making his good blunt face so dark?

Mr Elfoy explained their errand and asked if Muggins could get some men together to help in the gardens.

'I daresay, sir.'

'Clarissa bent forward in her saddle and held out her hand. 'Thank you Mr Muggins, it would be very good of you,' she said with her frank smile.

Muggins wiped his hand on his breeches before he shook it, somewhat reluctantly.

Mr Elfoy looked at the barn. 'You have been fixing the barn after all, I see Muggins,' he exclaimed.

Muggins drew himself up. 'I have Mr Elfoy, sir. I took the stone from the old Martin's farm, like I told you I would, even if I didn't have permission of the late Lord. The beasts cannot await permission.' He pronounced these words with an air of defiance looking latterly at Clarissa.

Elfoy was about to speak, but Clarissa interrupted.

'How sensible, Mr Muggins. I need just such a man who knows how to act on his own initiative to see to the garden. However, you must have much to do on the farm and you must not neglect it on my behalf.'

Ah, how good she is with these people, thought Oriana. How quickly she learns. She exchanged warm looks of approval with Elfoy.

'As to that ma'am, 'twould be a pleasure. My father would have been taken bad to see the grounds as they are.' He hesitated and looked at Clarissa with a flushed countenance, 'I should not have taken the stone, for it rightly belongs to you, ma'am. My mother tells me I'm not a patient man. Per'aps you would like to step down and meet her, miss. She'd be much honoured.'

The party dismounted and met Mrs Muggins, a round and cheery lady who regaled them with homemade scones and her own jam made only last year. As they sat in the cosy cottage, Clarissa heard tales of her mother's childhood when Mrs Muggins had been a maid in the great house.

At last they were able to leave and as they rode towards the house, Clarissa, who had been unusually silent' suddenly pulled up her horse and exclaimed, 'I have it. Mr Elfoy, I have it. Our encounter with Muggins has given me the answer to all of our problems.'

Oriana and Elfoy pulled up and looked at her in astonishment.

'The West Wing.'

Oriana said, 'I thought, my dear Clarissa, you had agreed with Mr Elfoy that the cost of repairing the West Wing is not to be thought of. I did not know that you had any desire to do so.'

'Of course I do not,' said Clarissa impatiently; 'We must sacrifice the West Wing entirely. It is of no use to me, but the stone and slate and timber might do proper repairs to cottages on the estate. It could do real good, instead of sitting uselessly at the edge of the house.'

Mr Elfoy's eyes lit up. Suddenly he could see a fast and reasonably inexpensive way to make the improvements his agent's heart desired. 'We could use the soldiers that have returned from the war to do the work. Many are wounded, but ... No. Consider, Miss Clarissa. The stone was imported by your grandfather at great cost - you would reduce the size of a great house...'

Clarissa interrupted, her eyes blazing with excitement. She turned to Oriana. 'Do *you* believe it could be done?'

Oriana considered. In the last days she and Clarissa had seen hardship on the estate that had touched their compassionate souls: so much needing done, but with so little funds to do it. Once acting as mistress of her father's estate, she had been shocked to see what had been allowed to happen here to the tenants all for the want of a little management. Though they could make do for the next year or so, she had felt all the evils for the tenants that having an impoverished mistress might bestow and had even thought of advising a sale to allay their suffering. Now, however, there was a real hope. 'I believe it could.'

The three galloped to the house talking of labour and architects and feeling, at last, that they might do something really fine for Clarissa's dependants.

When Oriana took a breath, she fell a little behind to observe the other two laughing and planning, Tristram Elfoy lit up with a passion to put wrongs right and the practical shrewdness to do so. She saw how Clarissa hung on his words and garnered his expertise, asking questions and matching him for enthusiasm. It was so rare to find a man share thoughts and plans so easily with a woman and Oriana wondered sadly if it was only his position as an employee that allowed this equality of ideas to bloom. Would he allow his wife to offer ideas as an equal? Something of Mr Elfoy's joy and warmth as he looked at Clarissa suddenly dispelled her cynicism.

Lord Staines had been delayed in paying his call to Clarissa by the arrival of unexpected guests. The Earl of Grandiston and the Honourable Charles Booth, to be precise. Staines and Booth had been at school together (though Staines had been the elder) and Grandiston was a man far too important in society not to be welcomed warmly to any home. They announced themselves to be passing from Grandiston's home further north on their way to London. Naturally, they were invited to stay and later to prolong their visit with some shooting and fishing on Lord Staines' tidy estate. Much to his surprise, both invitations were accepted and Staines imported this to his superior hospitality, as he confided to his mother.

His mother, resplendent today in a yellow gown and pink shawl, agreed with him faintly, 'Very likely, my dear. They do seem set to make a rather longer visit than I thought, though. Lord Grandiston has no height of manner, has he? He may be able to do you a great deal of good you know, with his relationship to the Royal Princes.'

'Indeed, by his reputation for pride he is much maligned. He has offered to introduce me at his club.'

However much Lady Staines may abhor gambling for large stakes she knew what a social coup it was for her son to be introduced to Watiers by someone of Grandiston's standing. 'My dear boy, you will be made socially. I daresay everyone will receive us.' She bustled off to see Cook about dinner feeling jubilant, but still with a nagging doubt as to their good fortune. Why should so great a man be at his leisure here when he had so little in common with her rather less brilliant son?

She received an inkling at dinner when she prattled on to cover her distress at the dreadful entrée (which had spoiled under the cook's anxiety about having to produce so many elegant dinners).

'We have a new neighbour at the Great House, gentlemen. A Miss Thorne is come into the estate after the sad death, so young, of her cousin the viscount. I believe that she has taken up residence there but we have not yet visited, have we my dear boy?'

Her son looked displeased. 'I do not believe that she is to be our neighbour. Indeed, her brother as good as sold the land to me. I consider it quite settled.'

Grandiston drawled, 'I do not believe her brother is the owner, or would not he have come into the property?'

Lady Staines was sometimes a silly woman but she had a woman's intuitions. Distinctly, under the drawl, she heard an interest in Grandiston's voice.

'No,' said her son, 'a half-brother, I believe. Not a noble family but quite respectable. As her nearest male relation, he naturally would be the one to guide her in what she must do. Her land would round mine off very nicely. It is my ambition to make Staines a Great Estate.'

'A worthy ambition, my dear fellow, you should lose no time in visiting the young lady. Perhaps we could accompany you on the morrow.'

'Are you acquainted with Miss Thorne, Lord Grandiston?'

'No indeed, Lady Staines, but I am always ready to make new acquaintance. It intrigues me, too, to meet a young lady who sets herself against her brother's wishes.'

Mr Booth, hearing the subtext in this, regarding Miss Petersham, gave a shout of laughter but upon the Earl's eye being cast his way, he controlled himself and apologized that his mind had wandered. Lady Staines watched and wondered.

Though they rode over the next day, they were denied entry by the imperturbable Sullivan. Lord Staines left his card and inquired to a morning when he might find the young lady at home.

'As to that, sir, I could not say. Miss Thorne is very much engaged with estate business at the moment.'

Staines was flustered whilst Grandiston admired the butler's style. He had just such an old retainer on his own estate.

'Estate business? Your mistress cannot mean to stay.'

Sullivan looked down his nose in a manner that suggested that Staines was of questionable respectability. He regally ignored the intrusive question and paused meaningfully, then said, 'I will deliver your card to my mistress, sir.'

'What a fine specimen of a butler,' declared Booth with great glee. 'Sent us about our business and no mistake. No disreputable characters will storm this castle. Wouldn't wager you buying this pile, Staines, she's settling in. Mark my words, sir, settling in.'

Oh, how I love you, Charles, thought Grandiston, observing his Lordship's affronted face. Pomposity withers in your presence.

His eyes had taken in the well-polished floor behind Sullivan and the signs of work beginning in the garden. The ladies were indeed settling in, and though Grandiston did not yet know if this was to his advantage, the landlord in him applauded their actions. Had they bitten off more than they could chew, however? Dawdling behind the rest, he contrived to ask a farm labourer the name and direction of the estate's agent.

Next day, Lord Staines received a perfectly civil note from Clarissa regretting that the house was not yet in a fit state to receive visitors and that she herself was too busy with important estate matters to call as yet. She thanked him for his visit and hoped he would be at home to renew it after, say, a month had elapsed.

This missive enraged Staines so much that despite his mother's entreaties, he dashed off a letter to her brother, castigating him for not exercising more control over his sister.

Returning home that evening after an interesting time spent in the Red Bull drinking his porter at the same time as Mr Elfoy's nightly ale, Grandiston accosted Charles in the hall.

'Charles, the bloom is once more upon your cheek. The country air agrees with you.'

'Grandiston. What are you about now?' said the Honourable Mr Booth with a wary look.

'Have you not thought, Charles, of your need, your quite *urgent* need, for a house in the country?'

Next day at breakfast, the gentlemen informed Lady Staines of their intention of leaving. Upon her protestations of grief, Mr Booth imparted some good news.

'Oh, ma'am, don't give it a thought. As a matter of fact I've taken a real fancy to this country. Best shooting I've had in an age. Mean to take a house in the neighbourhood. Be neighbours, you know.'

'But wherever can you mean to stay?' said the lady, faintly.

'Why the Dower House at Ashcroft, ma'am.'

CHAPTER 7

New Acquaintances

Lady Staines was determined, after the insouciance of this announcement by Mr Booth, to meet Miss Thorne who must, she felt, be at the bottom of his desire to stay in Hertfordshire.

She arrived at the door to be given the same message as her son at the hands of the stately Sullivan. However, his mother was made of sterner stuff.

'Of course, it is too early to intrude. Give her my regards and say I will call again.' She turned away with a faint smile, then turned back just as Sullivan had begun to shut the door. 'I feel a little faint in the heat of this spring day. So silly of me. Might I have a glass of water?' She put her delicate hand to her brow affectingly.

Sullivan bowed low and ushered her into the hall. He appreciated that he had met a match in the frail lady. 'Please take a seat in the library and I shall have someone attend you madam.'

Soon, Lady Staines was joined in the library by a fluttering lady of middle age wearing a dove-coloured silk dress and a lace cap decorated with a bewildering number of dove satin ribbons and carrying in a glass of water.

'My dear ma'am, so sorry to find you unwell, pray drink this,' said the lady and set about in a rather distracted way to plump some cushions and set the table nearer to Lady Staines' elbow.

'Miss *Thorne*?' she uttered.

The lady laughed, 'Oh, dear me no. I'm Miss Appleby, one of Miss Thorne's companions.' Then she looked distracted.

'*One* of her companions? She has more than one?' said Lady Staines, quite forgetting to sip her water.

'Three,' uttered Miss Appleby in fatalistic accents. 'That is to say two, I suppose, for Oriana is a friend bearing her company whilst Miss Micklethwaite and I are...Goodness, what am I saying? You are ill; you do not want to be hearing my ravings...'

Lady Staines remembered her illness with a jolt, though she did indeed want to listen to Miss Appleby. Her instinct for gossip was infallible.

Meanwhile, Miss Micklethwaite was intercepted on her way to the sitting room by Sullivan, who informed her that Lady Staines of Staines Manor was in the library.

'With Miss Appleby, Miss,' he added, significantly.

Miss Micklethwaite took it in at once. 'Good lord. What might not she say?' She hurried towards the library.

'Lady Staines, I am sorry to hear you are indisposed,' she said, 'I trust Louisa is taking good care of you.'

'Augusta, dear. Let me introduce you to Lady Staines. Your ladyship - Miss Augusta Micklethwaite.' Miss Appleby was relieved for she vaguely felt that she had not quite explained herself properly.

Lady Staines held out her hand to Miss Micklethwaite, '*Another* of Miss Thorne's companions, I presume?'

Miss Micklethwaite took up her seat with stolid serenity.

'Yes, indeed, Lady Staines. You find us a house full of women here. Miss Petersham bears Miss Thorne company. These young girls all have their particular friends, do they not? Miss Appleby here was the dearest friend of Mrs Thorne before she passed away and now stands somewhat in the nature of a mother to the young lady. I myself have been companion and teacher since she was a child and she could not bear to part with me, though she is too old for a governess now.'

Miss Appleby was amazed at Augusta's masterful summation: surrogate mother, governess and best friend, what could be more natural? It was, moreover, nearly the truth.

'Miss Thorne is very fortunate in her friends, I'm sure.' said Her Ladyship graciously, 'I'm so sorry to intrude, but I fear at my time of life, these attacks overcome one.'

The ladies disclaimed and offered her tea, which she accepted. Although they all enjoyed a chat, there were no more unguarded words. Miss Micklethwaite was a bit of a mystery. Just a touch less genteel than any governess she had encountered, she was nevertheless a woman of sense. Her manner to Lady Staines was respectful but untouched by any servility. Her more genteel companion showed more irritating attentions to her comfort but was clearly a lady. Though she lingered over tea, she had almost given up on her quarry, when suddenly Clarissa entered the room crying, 'We have a tenant for the Dower House.'

She broke off at the sight of Lady Staines and said all that was civil upon her introduction. She was wearing her new velvet riding dress (delivered that very day from the French emigrée dressmaker in Ashcroft village, who had cut it from her mother's opera cloak) with mannish epaulets and a rakish hat adorned with black gauze. She looked every bit a lady and she had a becoming flush upon her face and a sparkle in her eye.

As Clarissa minded her manners, Lady Staines shook her hand, apologized again for intruding, and left the house satisfied.

'If you want that land, Frederick, you would do well to marry the owner,' she recommended her son later that evening. 'It will cost you a great deal less and she is a very pretty girl.'

Whilst deprecating his mother's lack of delicacy in her remark, it gave Lord Staines food for thought. He was a very wealthy young man, owing to some fortunate investments of his father's, and did not seek to marry for any but social advancement. He already had an impoverished Earl's daughter in his eye, if he could just get over her rather unfortunate complexion. Miss Thorne's father may be no-one, but she *was* the granddaughter of a viscount and if she were passable ... It was with more patience that he awaited the allotted time to visit his new neighbour.

Mrs Cornelia Thorne, meanwhile, was shrieking at her husband about his decision to set off for Ashcroft.

'Oh, John, you cannot. It would delay my visit to Bath and I have so longed for the diversion.'

John was holding Staines' letter aloft, 'But, my dear, think. Clarissa is meaning to stay at Ashcroft. I can no longer place any dependence on her coming here. One would have thought that she would have given up this foolish start but she is setting the neighbourhood in a turmoil. I must go and order her home to us.'

'You may just as well tell her to come by letter. But it is not convenient for her to come for at least another month. I get so few chances to go to assemblies these days. Why, I have not had occasion to wear my new lilac silk since I bought it three months ago. It would be very well for Clarissa to stay at home and look after the children next year, but this year she would be sure to want to go Bath with us.' She saw that John was looking doubtful and she made haste to pet him, 'You are such a good brother, John. In a month, when we are returned to Bath, Clarissa will be more willing to see sense and follow your wise guidance.'

John returned his wife's caress and reluctantly agreed. 'But my dear one ... assemblies! I thought we meant to keep to private parties since the death of my stepmother. The mourning period is not quite over. It is not seemly.'

Cornelia pouted, 'Nonsense, John. It is not as though she were your mamma. I shall wear black gloves, of course, but we cannot still be in mourning for one who is not even a blood relation. It is six months.'

Mr Thorne salved his conscience with her argument and with the reflection that his stepmother was not well known in Bath and they might thus be spared the opprobrium of the sticklers of etiquette who resided there. He sat down to write a measured letter to his sister, adjuring her to come home to her brother and her fond sister-in-law and to give up her ridiculous attempt to set up her household with little money on a derelict estate. Her behaviour had already made her ridiculous to the district at large, as he had only today been informed by post. (That it had also rendered him ridiculous, he did not dwell upon). He would be absent from home for a month and after that time he would come to bring her to her new home. He would be accompanied by his lawyer with some papers to sign that would obviate the need for her to worry her head any longer with the millstone of her inheritance.

This letter had the effect of freezing Clarissa when it was delivered at breakfast that morning. She had been looking at her best again, with her hair dressed by the talented Becky and wearing a black muslin gown cut low at the bosom and kept decent by a gauze kerchief tucked into the bodice. Miss Micklethwaite's face rarely lost its grim expression but she was well satisfied with the bloom that a busy and useful life had put onto Clarissa's face and was now shocked to see her face turn pale as she clutched her letter.

Miss Appleby noticed too and flustered, 'My dear girl, whatever is the matter?'

Clarissa looked distracted and upon Miss Micklethwaite's blunt interjection, 'that brother of yours,' she merely held out the letter for her to read. This Miss Micklethwaite did with deliberation, a darker than ever look upon her face. She grasped Clarissa's hand firmly.

'A month is a long time, my dear. Look what we have already achieved.'

Clarissa searched her face for reassurance, but her heart was heavy. These last days when all the ladies worked and laughed together, the plans they had still to realize had become as dear to her as anything she had ever known. It had salved the grief of her parents' death and she was moreover sure that they would be proud of her. Her mother, influenced by the words of Mary Wollstonecraft, had seen women's independence as a right and had despised the selling of women into the career of marriage even where there was no equality of intelligence or values.

Somewhere, though, Clarissa had been expecting this. Women's freedom was not always won even by money. It could all be taken away, even now.

'Oh dear,' said Miss Appleby, despairingly, as she read the letter, 'We are undone. If only you had a husband to protect you, my dear girl.'

'Louisa!' rebuked Miss Micklethwaite. But it was too late; Clarissa had run from the room.

Augusta Micklethwaite was a strong woman but she did not underestimate how weak that was when faced by the power of the male establishment. She had previously had employment in a school run by a deserted wife, in order to support her family which had nevertheless had to close when the husband had insisted that it was an insult to him as a gentleman. That his destitute family was not a worse insult was something that Augusta could not understand or forgive. She still sent her late mistress what money she could spare.

Now, she thought that little as she liked to ask for his help, she needed her brother's advice for Clarissa. He was a fair man and what help he could render he would. Had it not been for his foolish marriage to the merchant's petted daughter, Augusta might have accepted his offer of a home before now. As it was, Augusta's tongue and Clara's false airs did not mix. She wrote to her brother, but she was not hopeful. As her male next of kin, John might claim guardianship of his sister and then he could do as he chose. Clarissa's age was against her.

All of this she confided to Oriana as she awaited Clarissa in the green room after breakfast. Oriana was wearing her navy velvet riding habit whose severe lines she had chosen for their plainness. Her hair was simply looped as usual and her mannish hat was adorned only with a muslin veil, which could be drawn across her face to shield her from insects. Her attempts to disguise her charms were wasted. The high-necked velvet robe was a beautiful frame for her face and figure. Augusta was quite as concerned for her as for Clarissa. She was a creature made for passionate love, but one who might yet be sold in marriage to an inferior man or live a life of drudgery to avoid the unwanted attention she must forever excite. Yet where could there be an equal to this fabulous creature? Only a man with intelligence and passion to match her own. Miss Micklethwaite thought poorly of the male sex and could not think of a specimen of it that would be equal to the task.

Oriana was saying, 'Poor Clarissa. I was hoping that her sister-in-law's jealous humours might be enough to stop Mr Thorne pursuing her. We've all been living in a fool's paradise. Just when we have the new income from the Dower House tenant. Three times the rent we were expecting, Mr Elfoy told me. Do you know who took it? Clarissa did not tell me.'

'No, indeed, my dear. I fear Lady Staines' visit discommoded her. Perhaps my brother can help. If we can at least delay, perhaps some worthy gentlemen might come along who supports her object here,' said Miss Micklethwaite.

Oriana laughed ironically, 'Waity, not you adjuring a good marriage as well as Appleby and the rest of the world.'

'I work with the world as it is, my dear. I do not believe marriage to be the only rational pursuit for a woman, yet I do not despise the love and family life that a *good* marriage gives a woman. Elfoy is a fine young man with an obvious attraction for Clarissa, if he but had the connections to protect her - but it is not to be thought of.'

'No, indeed it would be just such a connection that her brother must fear and may even use his power to break ...'

Sullivan announcing Mr Elfoy, coming as usual to ride with the ladies and look at the progress of their plans, interrupted her.

He bowed over Miss Micklethwaite's hand and then turned to Oriana, 'Work has begun on draining the top field and I thought we might begin there today. It was a very good notion of yours, Miss Petersham. My attention was taken too much by the tenant's troubles to notice the possibility. Muggins has organized the other farmers into a work party.

He is a splendid fellow. I do not know where he gets his energy from.'

Oriana blushed at the compliment. 'It is only that my father made a great deal of money by doing the same at my home. It improved the yields he said. We shall have to find a way to further reward Muggins.'

Mr Elfoy's face took on a soft look. 'He can be a difficult man, but Miss Thorne totally won him over. She is a remarkable young lady, do you not think?'

'I have always thought so,' said Miss Micklethwaite dampeningly. It would not do to encourage him. Mr Elfoy was aware of betraying himself and looked studiously at the carpet.

At this point Clarissa entered the room, still wearing her muslin dress, her eyes suspiciously pink. She wore a resolute expression, however and she said in an even tone, 'Mr Elfoy, will you marry me?'

CHAPTER 8

Hearts and Tenants

There was a stunned silence then Miss Micklethwaite let out a sharp 'Clarissa!' in a tone that Clarissa had not heard since she had spilled ink carelessly in the schoolroom. Her heart had been beating fast since she had opened her mouth. It had seemed simple and easy to explain her thoughts to Mr Elfoy who had come to be her friend. She had kept her eyes on his face with a semblance of calm however, and saw how stupidly she had been mistaken. His face flushed with humiliation, he looked like a man who had been offered an insult of the most grievous kind. Waity's voice brought her to her senses - whatever her troubles, how could she expect this excellent young man to give up all hope of domestic happiness for financial gain? Her composure crumpled, 'I - I'm so sorry,' she cried as she ran from the room.

Mr Elfoy took up his hat from the side table, stiff as any marionette. 'Excuse me ladies,' he said punctiliously, 'I must be going.'

Oriana grabbed at his arm 'Please, dear Mr Elfoy. Let us explain. Clarissa is overset. It is all the fault of a letter we received this morning.'

'Indeed sir,' Miss Micklethwaite added, 'You must hear us out.'

And so Mr Elfoy let himself be coaxed to sit down and recovered himself as the ladies explained about Thorne's orders and Clarissa's fear of being ousted from Ashcroft. He listened and felt his humiliation recede as his understanding grew – he began to feel pity for the ladies' plight.

Presently he went and found Clarissa pulling leaves from a rosebush in a distracted way. She was in a little arbour near the house that had been rediscovered as the men had pulled apart the neglected brush around it. She looked at once so miserable and so beautiful that Mr Elfoy had to check the instincts of a man in love and take her into his arms. For such he was, as Clarissa's question had shown him. He had hidden his true feelings even from himself until that moment when he was offered what he could never have hoped for and at the same second realized that he could not take it. Now Clarissa sat, pulling at the silly leaves, her large eyes liquid with tears, her head drooped disconsolately.

'Miss Thorne,' he said gently, joining her on the arbour seat. Clarissa started and turned her face so that he might not see that she had been crying. She dashed away a tear from her cheek and said with her usual impulsiveness, 'Oh, Mr Elfoy, I never meant to ... to ...'

'Miss Petersham explained ...'

'I am so sorry, Mr Elfoy, it is my stupid tongue that gets me into these awful scrapes. It is just that my only hope seems to be to marry - and we have become such good friends ... It is not that I wish to marry, though I have never met a gentleman I would rather ... But I did not give thought to your feelings, except it would make you master of Ashcroft and I know how you love it and maybe you wouldn't so much mind being married for that, but I should have known ...'

With one hand Mr Elfoy took both of Clarissa's (which were engaged in pulling apart a rose leaf as she had made her embarrassed speech) and with the other he turned her face towards his. Her eyes lowered but suddenly joined his clear good green eyes when he tilted her chin.

'If I could help you by ...' Clarissa put up her hand to hush him, overcome with embarrassment, '... but I could not. I wish ... that is ... it is not possible ...'

The tears spilled over Clarissa's eyes as she looked into his grave eyes, too spellbound to look away.

'But it won't do Clarissa,' he said, unconsciously using her name, 'Marriage to such as I is exactly the thing your brother would despise and just such a marriage as he could dissolve. You have done me the great honour to say you have not met another gentleman whom you would rather marry ...' he said gently while she blushed and uttered an inarticulate sound '... but your acquaintance is not large. Soon you will meet many gentlemen and you will find one to love who can offer you that equality of position that I cannot. We will speak no more of this. It would not serve for either of us.'

'Yes, it was appalling of me. Please let us forget it,' murmured Clarissa, with a semblance of calm returning. She raised her hand to his in a gesture of farewell, and as he held it and stooped over it, she looked shyly at his face, trying for her old good humour. But her hand trembled at his touch; he flushed and moved away swiftly.

Clarissa sat, radiant and alive where she had sat so dejectedly before. He too had trembled and in a different way to that of a shy young man. She hardly dared to think why or the reason for her own beating heart. No doubt proximity to a young gentleman like Mr Elfoy was enough to overcome any young lady so untutored in the ways of the world as she. But the power of knowing that she had affected him.

'For someone whose offer of marriage has just been refused, Clarissa, your spirits are bearing up well,' she said to herself. Then she laughed a pure clear laugh that brought Miss Appleby running towards her.

'I have just been trying to find you child. Why, whatever is so funny?'

'Nothing Appleby, only, I've just had an offer of marriage refused,' and she was led away by her concerned friend, unable to stop herself from smiling and quite unable to explain why.

Meanwhile, Tristram Elfoy was riding away in a turmoil of emotions, a state of affairs unusual for him. He was the only son of a devoted mother who had been brought up to esteem his noble heritage (his uncle was a baronet) and understand the realities of his position in the world. He had accompanied his cousin on a trip to Europe (sadly truncated due to the troubles on the continent) and felt himself to be fortunate in his relatives, without the least bit of resentment at his lack of funds. He had taken the job of estate manager with the intention of supporting his mother more comfortably. Indeed, his annual wage provided a variety of comforts to his respectable cottage home. He was a good son, a hard worker and of temperate habits. He enjoyed his life and had henceforth dealt with the challenges of his life with cheerfulness, resolution and acuity; but though he liked himself well enough he knew that he had no right to dream of the mistress of Ashcroft. His heart was repelled by so uneven a match, for he would seek to take care of his wife not to be her pensioner. Yet here he was with the vision of Clarissa's mouth burned into his soul and the fire of his love coursing around his veins in a way that his head was seeking to throttle unto death.

What is it about her that has me spellbound? he asked himself. Her face and manner, so impish and impulsive, so different from his own placidity; her gentle goodness in all her dealings, especially with those beneath her, her swift intelligence that met his equally, all these things had made her haunt his dreams.

'Oh, Clarissa!' he cried to the wind as he rode through Ashcroft park. He felt himself to be in the grip of a passion that burned with all the fire of his heart and that must as swiftly be quenched. 'I must not think of her.'

Thus it was that he was unaware of the carriage coming through the gate of the park until he was hailed.

'Mr Elfoy, well met,' called The Honourable Charles Booth, 'Hold up.'

Tristram pulled in his horse and touched his hand to his hat respectfully. 'Gentlemen, can I be of assistance?' He hoped that his flushed countenance and his beating heart were not apparent to Mr Booth and his noble companion, Lord Grandiston.

'You said there will be stabling enough for the carriage horses and the hacks - give directions to my man will you?'

'Certainly, sir. I've had the house made ready for you. I believe your valet took charge, My Lord, he arrived last night.'

Grandiston brushed his sleeve with a languid hand and said, 'Yes, I know. I had to dress myself this morning. I wonder whether I dare meet his fastidious eye?'

Mr Elfoy found himself grinning appreciatively as his eye ran over Grandiston's immaculate person, 'I think you're safe, sir.'

'I should say so,' said his companion, 'Elegant as a Bond Street Beau.'

'Do you think so, Charles?' said Lord Grandiston hopefully, 'The height of my ambition. I'm sure we must all bow to your judgement. And yet ....' And he raised his quizzing glass to look balefully at Booth's waistcoat. At his friend's inarticulate objections, Grandiston turned his singularly sweet smile on Mr Elfoy; 'You must ignore my young friend, sir. He is given to sartorial delusions of grandeur. We'll see you in the park no doubt.'

Mr Elfoy directed the groom and then rode on, chuckling at the new Dower House residents. Mr Booth he thought of as a likeable young cub (although he was but a few years his junior) but Grandiston was more difficult. He affected boredom and lethargy, but Elfoy saw the steel and energy behind the pose. Not a man to cross, his lordship, but he had warm, humorous eyes that showed no height of manner. A man born to command - but one who led with light reins.

'An excellent fellow, Elfoy, don't you think Hugo? I only wish my father's agent were as efficient. He's a doddery old fool; been around since doomsday, so we can't fob him off.'

'Isn't it time you set about running Fenway yourself?'

Charles flushed but recovered his insouciance, 'M'father thinks it inappropriate to accept the help of Bond Street wasters such as m'self, old fellow, so I keep well clear, except when my mama and sisters are at home.'

His lordship laid a delicate arm on the younger man's shoulders, 'Your father says a great deal more than he means, Charles. A libertine, yes - but not yet a waster.'

Mr Booth gave a crack of laughter, 'Well, if you're going to give me the name of libertine then I'd best get started. I hope the cellar is decent in this place.'

The coach had arrived at its destination. McIntosh, his lordship's valet, was awaiting the gentlemen on the steps. His eye travelled Grandiston's person, but he did not shudder, a sign that bode well.

'Mr Booth is inquiring about the claret, McIntosh. Is it tolerable?' he drawled as he languidly mounted the stairs.

'Unfortunately sir, the lady who was in residence here for many years was of an abstemious nature. She had everything but ratafia removed from the cellars, sir.'

The Honourable Charles stopped dead, 'Ratafia? Good God, Grandiston. Why did you bring me to this god-forsaken place?' he exclaimed in horror.

Macintosh's dour Caledonian features lightened slightly, 'I anticipated some discrepancies in the cellar, my lord, and brought an extra coach for the wine. I trust you have no objection to the extra expense, sir?' he inquired of his master.

Charles cut in, 'No, no, McIntosh. 'He said expansively, 'Think nothing of it.'

CHAPTER 9

Old Friends

The ladies were in the morning room after breakfast. Clarissa had slept like a baby and felt herself to be repressing a burst of happiness such as she had seldom known. All rational reflection of the difficulties that now confronted her could not extinguish the hope that lay beyond sense. Everything was possible, everything. None of the representations of logic that her more serious side put forward could cloud the joy of one thing. Mr Elfoy had trembled.

There had been no reference made to Clarissa's absurd behaviour of last night – highly-strung nerves, thought Miss Appleby. The dearest girl had been through so much. She looked doubtfully at her this morning. Her hair was dressed in the new way that she had adopted, she wore the dove-coloured muslin with an air, trimmed as it was with the fine white gauze fichu tucked into the low-cut bodice and held with her mama's round pearl circlet. Her eyes sparkled and her curls shone in a way that transformed the colour from mouse to a dazzling melee of hues in blonde and chestnut. Why, if she had not been aware of the facts she would have thought Clarissa looked quite, well, happy. She could not forbear exclaiming, 'Why Clarissa my dear, you look quite radiant today. I thought that the letter from your brother might bring you down.'

Clarissa looked serious for a moment but then her sunny smile returned, 'I cannot think at the moment, but I am sure that I shall think of some way of rebuffing him. It's not today in any event, and we still have a great deal to do. I think we should continue as normal until we get advice from Mr Micklethwaite. It may not be so bad after all.'

Miss Micklethwaite exchanged glances with Oriana, both of whom had some notion of the reasons for Clarissa's sudden optimism. They would need to keep harder heads about the impending disaster, but they silently assented by looks to keep their inevitable reflections to themselves for the present.

'Well,' she said rising, 'then I had better get along to the kitchens. The stillroom is in need of reordering.'

Clarissa's voice stopped them, 'No, Waity, don't go. I quite forgot to tell you at breakfast but Sullivan delivered a note from Mr Elfoy. It's the Dower House tenants. He's bringing them over this morning to be introduced.'

The ladies exclaimed and asked for details but whilst Clarissa was replying the morning room door flew open and Sullivan announced, 'His Lordship, the Earl of Grandiston; The Honourable Mr Charles Booth and Mr Elfoy, Miss.'

The gentlemen were on the threshold; Miss Petersham turned sharply; she gave a little cry, then, 'Grandiston!' and she flew across the room, her arms extended to catch both of his in hers, 'Oh, Grandiston!'

Grandiston caught her hands and looked down into her eyes, shining with a warmth that he had seldom seen in her except when she had looked at her father. She looked so beautiful, even with her hair in that constricted style. She looked like an angel and caught off-guard, Grandiston returned her look and for a moment his suavity slipped and the real man showed his face. The ladies therefore saw him at his very best; the harsh looking face softened, the eyes humorous and warm, bending down to Oriana from his considerable height.

'Oh Grandiston,' she said again, 'you cannot think how I have longed to see you. You are the nearest thing to my father that I have left.'

Miss Micklethwaite, interestedly watching this encounter with the rest of the room's occupants, thought she saw the giant retreat a little at this. He bowed over her hands and kissed them however and said, 'Miss Petersham, Oriana, how do you come to be here?'

Oriana withdrew her hands and coloured a little. 'You did not know?'

'No, indeed,' said Grandiston, 'I have just come to stay with my friend who has become tenant in the Dower House. You know Mr Booth, I believe?'

Oriana looked dazedly beyond him to his companion; the handsome, merry faced young man brought back memories of her horrible London season. She did not know why her spirits had suddenly sank except that she had thought that, that - but what? That her father would come in behind him slapping his back and shouting for his breakfast after a long ride? That Grandiston could whisk her away to a time when she had been happy and secure before she had to worry about whether Fitzroy or Clarissa's brother could rule her life? That he would keep looking at her in that teasing way of his ...

'Mr Booth. We met in London, of course,' she said, extending her hand. He bowed over it and swept a magnificent leg much in the manner of gallants from the previous generation, 'Your devoted slave, ma'am.'

Clarissa giggled. This had the effect of drawing the gentlemen's gazes in her direction. Booth looking a little discomfited.

'Oh, dear. Excuse me, if you will,' said Clarissa, still smiling.

'Ladies,' said Oriana smoothly, 'may I introduce Lord Grandiston, an old and dear friend of my father, and his friend The Honourable Charles Booth. This is Miss Clarissa Thorne, our hostess, and the Misses Micklethwaite and Appleby who, like me, are bearing her company here at Ashcroft.'

His Lordship held out his hand to the young lady who hardly looked old enough to be anyone's hostess, then bowed over the hand of the little reed of a lady who fluttered in her beribboned frock. This gallantry almost overset her and she exclaimed and tinkled her little laugh whilst she waved her lace handkerchief to fan her reddened cheek. Clarissa giggled again and caught Grandiston's ironical eye as he observed these transports. They had only just subsided when Mr Booth had the office of touching her hand and she was off again. Lord Grandiston's eyebrow went up and Clarissa gave herself to a helpless fit of the giggles. His Lordship had himself in hand until he turned to Miss Micklethwaite.

'Fool,' remarked that lady, 'Well, that'll teach you young men to keep it to a nod next time or we'll all be driven to Bedlam by Louisa's foolishness.'

Meeting Oriana's eye this time, he felt his restraint go and soon all five of the young company were helpless with laughter, though Miss Appleby was unsure what the joke was, and Miss Micklethwaite's face remained composed.

The arrival of refreshment brought some order but the whole company had left formality behind and so instead of quelling Mr Booth's fulsome compliments with her usual frigidity, Oriana merely grinned or groaned, depending on his deftness. She thought of him as a silly boy and she divided herself between fending him off and chatting with the rest of the company. She could not help her gaze resting fondly on Grandiston from time to time for his presence was giving this time a kind of magic from her past, when she was the favourite daughter of a great man ruling the roost in a great house. Grandiston she saw, was mightily entertained by Clarissa - who looked, thought Oriana, so vivacious and pretty today. She was conscious of a twinge of something strange. Probably I want my old friend all to myself, she thought, at least until I have caught up with him. Mr Elfoy was asking her something; she had to ask him to repeat it.

Elfoy was enjoying the camaraderie that had been so easily established, and smiled at Booth's outrageous attempts at flattering Miss Petersham whilst suffering agonies when he heard Clarissa laugh at one of Grandiston's dry remarks. Of course he had expected that she would have found an admirer, just not so ridiculously soon. He saw Grandiston admire the circlet at her breast, saw her move the ringlet which had fallen over her shoulder so that he could better see, and burned.

Clarissa was enjoying herself more each moment. She did not see that she was flirting with Grandiston, for her knowledge of the ways of the world was small. Yesterday had filled her with such a wonderful confidence that her heart sang and she was at her prettiest. Her companions were the best in the world: she thought Grandiston devilishly attractive and charming and Booth the greatest of young bloods. She had never been in such male company before and she was relishing it - men who, like her father, were just as pleasant as women. But although she seldom looked at him, it was Elfoy for whom her heart sang and as he bent to listen to Miss Appleby she thought, 'Tristram.'

Waity watched it all whilst occasionally replying to remarks made to her with her usual acerbity. When she told the Honourable Charles (upon hearing his well-turned compliments to Oriana) that if his mother did not know how to deal with that sort of behaviour, she did, he gave a bark of laughter and declared himself her slave. 'When you threw my hat into the mud the first time I met you my fear has held me in your sway.'

'At the Inn. That was you. I knew then that you were a reprobate and I haven't changed my opinion.'

She liked them, though she would never have openly declared it. Booth is after Oriana, and I could have sworn that Grandiston's hers. Now he's flirting outrageously with Clarissa whilst Elfoy and Oriana look, well ... what? They are getting themselves into a pretty pickle. She looked at Grandiston. I could trust a man with that jaw to get me out of many straits, but matters of the heart? Well, I'll step in if needs be, if only we can send this brother of Clarissa's packing. She looked at Miss Appleby fluttering her eyelashes and her handkerchief in equal time. Oh, Louisa, aware of no more than her own beating heart.

'Why do you take the Dower House, Mr Booth?' inquired Clarissa presently.

Grandiston achieved an interested expression, 'Yes why *is* that Charles?'

Mr Booth ignored him, 'An inveterate love of the country, Miss Thorne,' he said jovially but untruthfully. Since even his country buckskins and top boots bore the cut of the best town tailor, not to mention the daringly nifty yellow waistcoat that he sported today, this was a little surprising to the ladies.

'But do I not remember that your family own a great estate in Yorkshire, sir?' asked Oriana.

'Well, yes ma'am, that is to say, well ...It is a little far from town. I can travel to London from here in a day's ride in case business should call me.'

'Ah,' said Clarissa, still mystified 'I see. Well, I hope you will be very happy here.'

There could be no doubt of that. When the gentlemen took their leave they had stayed for a full hour beyond the polite twenty minutes allotted for a morning call and they had agreed to Clarissa's invitation for dinner that evening. When a chance remark by Miss Appleby announced the younger ladies' habit of taking a walk after their light luncheon, the gentlemen elected to come back later and accompany them.

Oriana had to wait for three hours before her chance to talk to Grandiston presented itself. She dropped her shawl and he retrieved it so that they fell a little behind the others. She was a little stiff, though she had no idea why until Grandiston said gently, 'You may have misunderstood me earlier. When I came back from the Peninsular and heard the news of your father, I sought you out at once. Your brother would not give me your direction.'

She turned to him and her eyes shone, 'I knew I could not have been mistaken in you,' she said impulsively. 'He did not want our acquaintance to know I had become a school teacher.' She saw his eyebrows rise at this intelligence and her eyes teased him, 'I assure you I was *very* good and patient. My humble position quelled my rebellious spirit so that in all the time I was at Clarissa's mother's school, I didn't kill even *one* of our young ladies.'

'Now that does surprise me, remembering your lamentable temper,' he quipped back. His voice became more serious. 'It must have been difficult to change your position so radically,' Grandiston said gently. Almost without thought Oriana drew her arm through his as she had used to.

'Far, far, more difficult to stay at home.' Though she had attempted to speak jauntily, her voice cracked, and she knew that she would die if she gave way.

'Yes, I see. Your brother does not improve with acquaintance,' he said so silkily that she was obliged to laugh and in doing so composed herself.

'Dreadful man. It was father's fault, I think; Fitz always knew that Papa despised him. Perhaps if he had taken more pains with him - but he was such a sulky boy that Papa couldn't abide it. I don't blame him now - but I cannot live with him.'

Grandiston played for a moment with his quizzing glass which hung from his waistcoat; 'It seemed you had for a time another home in the offing. Were you not engaged to be married?'

He was looking at her keenly as he said this and her pride was hurt. Did he too believe her capable of that grotesque engagement? The anger flickered over her face to be replaced by the ice. 'We found we did not suit,' she said baldly. 'Shouldn't we quicken the pace to catch up the others?'

Grandiston wished that she would confide in him, but Oriana had always been proud and impulsive. Surely it was this spirit that made it impossible for her to live at home, or take up any of the offers of marriage she had no doubt received in her London season. Was this wilfulness selfish and careless, or was it the true pride of independence? He would not have thought her capable of the fickle act of a broken engagement, so sure had she always been of her own mind. Perhaps, though, he had not really known the spoiled daughter of an adoring father as well as he had thought. Maybe he too, like her other suitors, had been captivated by her beauty.

They joined the others and he began to regale Clarissa with tales of Oriana's young girlhood, her imperious fury with her first pony when it had thrown her, her father's equal fury at her behaviour. Though Oriana remained a little stiff at first, eventually she laughed and threatened to tell much worse stories about him.

The ladies got back to the house a great deal later than usual and got very little done before dinner ushered their friends back again.

'This will never do,' chattered Clarissa happily, 'we must ban the gentlemen from our walk tomorrow or we shall never get on with our estate business.'

'Indeed, yes,' said Oriana teasingly, 'we mustn't neglect Mr Elfoy.'

Clarissa blushed and ran up the stairs to dress.

CHAPTER 10

Confidences and Plots

The ladies had taken pains in their toilette that evening. Oriana was encouraged to wear one of the dresses that her old butler had sent from home, a light blue silk cut very low at the bodice over an under-dress of muslin, embroidered with tiny white roses. She rearranged her hair letting some of the magnificent curls cluster as they wished around her beautiful patrician face. Grandiston should at least see that she was her father's daughter still.

Clarissa came in whilst she was bestowing a frothy lace shawl about her shoulders and gasped.

'Oh, my dear Oriana, you look beautiful,' she gasped. It was said so naturally that Oriana laughed lightly.

'Perhaps I need no longer be a school mistress – at least until your brother comes.' She was quite sorry that she had spoken, since Clarissa's radiance dimmed somewhat. 'Forget

I said anything. Tonight we are neither of us school mistresses, I think.'

Her black silk, adorned as it was with her mother's fine lace, looked so well that Clarissa knew herself to be in her best looks. The time was coming to leave off mourning for her mother, but it would be seemly for another few months to wear little colour in respect for her unknown cousin whose heiress she had become.

The ladies left the room in high spirits and found the three gentlemen there (for Mr Elfoy had also been invited) very much at their ease with the ladies. Miss Micklethwaite had distinguished the occasion with the addition of her finest Paisley shawl (a present from her wealthy brother) whereas Miss Appleby's dress was adorned by a multitude of lace and gauze shawls held in place, thought Clarissa wickedly, by every piece of jewellery that she owned.

The entrance of the younger ladies was everything they could have wished. Mr Booth gave a start and said, 'By Jove.' He grasped Oriana's hand and pelted her with so many inarticulate compliments that she was obliged to laugh.

'Miss Petersham, you look ... you've never looked lovelier ... that is to say, your gown ... your hair ...'

'Your address, Charles, leaves us all standing,' interjected Grandiston smoothly, 'however, do surrender the lady's hand.' He grasped it himself and bowed low over it, murmuring, 'Charles says it all for me.' At his touch, Miss Petersham blushed slightly and uncharacteristically, her eyes glowing. He passed swiftly onto Miss Thorne, however, and before Mr Booth reclaimed her, she had the happiness of seeing him say something to her friend that made her giggle. She was very sure that she was glad that two of her dearest friends stood on such easy terms with each other, but she sincerely hoped (for her own good) that Clarissa was not developing into a flirt.

Mr Elfoy greeted the ladies with his customary good manners. He could not but be aware of the change in Miss Petersham and he gave her a simple compliment on her looks, but his demeanour to Miss Thorne was a little reserved, Oriana thought.

Actually, he was in turmoil. Would Clarissa ever stop getting prettier each time he saw her? What did she mean by it? She was too kind to torment him, so why did she smile so and laugh with Grandiston? It seemed his Lordship was growing particular in his attentions and Tristram thought that he should be glad that Clarissa had found such a suitable suitor. He was glad – or would be, in time.

Had either of the young ladies had any pretensions to social climbing, their duennas might have given them embarrassment. As it was, they enjoyed Miss Appleby's fascinating flirtation with the earl and his companion. Mr Elfoy had not enough of the town bronze about him to send her fluttering (good gracious, thought Oriana, can that really be a *fan?*) and blushing by turn. The young ladies and gentlemen watched fascinated as Miss Appleby wafted fan and eye lashes in a captivating display of arts from a bygone age of courtship. She was arch and playful by turns and it was only when The Honourable Charles was rapped on the knuckles after addressing to her a perfectly innocent request for the salt that Miss Micklethwaite was moved to intervene.

'Louisa, strive not to be a fool.'

Much to Grandiston's chagrin (for he had enjoyed the little spectacle) Miss Appleby promptly collapsed, like a stuck balloon. As the lively dinner conversation continued she recovered under the kind and unalarming gentlemanliness of Mr Elfoy.

It was not usual, but seemed perfectly natural that the topic of Mr Thorne's imminent arrival and its likely outcome was discussed in front of the gentlemen. Mr Booth was full of easy sympathy and sadness at the ways of the world. Grandiston, however, asked to be told a little bit about the gentleman.

Clarissa obliged. 'There is not much to tell. He left home ten years ago and was given his portion from my father at that time. I have seen him very occasionally since then,' she paused and flushed a little, 'he did not really approve of my mother, you see. She was too free in her thoughts and actions for him. His reaction to her and papa was to become ultra-respectable as I believe his own mother had been. He certainly did not approve of the way they brought me up, free to speak my mind. He often said to father I was educated beyond my sex.' She stopped here and became a little conscious.

Charles interjected cheerfully, 'Not at all. You don't seem at all bookish to me. Not like those terrible women at the literary luncheons my mother gives who creep up on one and ask if I think Sophocles was right. It leaves one completely bug-eyed.'

Your conversation, Charles, though always diverting, is not always useful,' said Grandiston quelling. 'Won't you continue, Miss Thorne?'

Clarissa laughed and blushed, 'I'm afraid, Mr Booth, that we ladies are all frightfully bookish and have even been known to talk about Sophocles over luncheon,' – Mr Booth looked shocked – 'but not to young gentlemen who might not enjoy it.'

'That's all right then,' said Mr Booth, relieved.

'Charles.' admonished Grandiston despairingly.

Clarissa continued, 'Now my brother, though not fond of me, I think, wishes to give me a home. He believes that though perfectly surrounded by chaperones, I am not fit to be left alone.'

Miss Appleby interjected clutching Grandiston's arm, 'I cannot but think he is also moved by motives of gain. For his offer of a home was never so pressed after her dear mother first died. It was only after her cousin died and left the estate...'

Miss Micklethwaite's no nonsense tones interjected. 'Naturally, being an ignorant male of the usual sort,' - here her baleful eye ran over the assembled gentlemen, in case they should protest; none of them did – 'he holds that females are unable to run their own affairs. In spite of her superior education, Clarissa's youth might have inclined me to agree in this case. However, that scheming wench he's married will make her life a misery if she goes there *and* she'll find a way to line her pockets, or I'm a kipper.'

Mr Booth felt that this extraordinary statement required some sort of rebuff (to the effect, perhaps, that she left no odour of fish?), made a strangled sound and was relieved when Miss Micklethwaite swept on.

'They are social climbers, both of them, and I cannot stomach people who pretend to more than their situation in life. That, of course, is why young John could not stomach my dear Mrs Thorne. She was the daughter of a viscount, brought up in this very house in its heyday and had no need to adopt airs or worry over her respectability. She was a great lady and she could not but show it, even in a schoolhouse.' Her eyes grew misty, but she shook off the weakness that she detested and continued, 'If it were better for Clarissa to go to her brother, I can speak for all of us here in wishing for it. We are ready to leave whenever it is necessary. But, my lord, if you have any suggestions to avoid this, I should be pleased if you would speak.'

Every one of the ladies was astounded that Miss Micklethwaite should ask the opinion of the despised sex. Her reliance on Grandiston was unheralded and must be from some instinct that ran deep after such a relatively short acquaintance. However, Miss Appleby was sure such a tall man must have the answers, Miss Petersham had reason to know and trust him and Miss Thorne shared the same instincts, so they turned uncritical gazes on him and awaited his words.

If Grandiston was aware of the irony of the situation, thought Mr Elfoy, he gave no sign. It was his custom to command and Elfoy found himself awaiting his words as hopefully as the ladies.

They had by this time retired to the drawing room and Grandiston stood by the fire, one hand on the mantle above him very much at ease.

'It seems to me that you need to be busy getting to know your neighbours. Perhaps if you can establish yourself a little in the community it will be that much more difficult to dislodge you. If he feels the acceptance of the local gentry of your position here he may find upsetting them gives him pause.'

'I have long wished to welcome those of our neighbours who have called, but Sullivan has thus far denied us, until we could put the house and garden a little in order,' said Miss Appleby.

'You have all done a splendid job of it and it now behoves you to take your place in society.'

'Yes,' said Oriana, 'But will it serve, my Lord? Mr Thorne need not care for the opinions of this restricted neighbourhood when he lives so distant.'

Grandiston smiled. 'Indeed. Is it so restricted? The son of a baronet has just leased your Dower House ...'

'And has an earl to stay,' finished Mr Booth. 'Dashed bad form to puff up your consequence, Hugo.'

'Isn't it just? But I get the feeling, from what the ladies have said, that the more we puff up our consequence in Mr Thorne's presence the better off it might be. If he sees a way into more elevated company, perhaps ...'

'Trust Sullivan for that,' interjected Miss Micklethwaite.

'Oh dear,' sighed Clarissa, 'How dreadfully vulgar this all is, but I can't help thinking you're right, sir. He's a dreadful snob. He was so delighted when Juliana Sowersby befriended me when I came to stay with him last year. She's the daughter of the finest family in his village and a sweet girl. Cornelia was furious because she'd never been invited to the Manor.'

'Sowersby? Is that old Jonas Sowersby's heiress? I never met her,' said Charles.

'I did,' said Grandiston unexpectedly, 'She was at Almack's a number of times this season. Charming girl.'

'That explains it. Never go there - devilish dull place. Had to squire my sisters there until they got engaged. Don't care what you did in the Peninsular, Hugo, braving a night with my mother and sisters at Almack's and being obliged to dance with m'mother's friends, well, *I* should get a medal.'

'Quite, Charles; however, we are considering the best advice to give Miss Thorne at the moment. Why don't you invite Miss Sowersby to stay? The season is ending and she might be free to visit on her way further north, don't you think?'

'What a good idea. If Juliana were to be here when John arrived he should at least take care how he spoke to me. He would not order me to pack my bags at once, which I live in dread of him doing. But, will she come ...?'

'Another thing, my Lord,' interrupted Mr Elfoy, 'If Sullivan begins to admit callers then my Lord and Lady Staines will no doubt appear. That may not be to Miss Thorne's advantage, since Lord Staines had desired to buy the estate and had indeed arranged something of the sort with Mr Thorne.'

'You did not tell me that, sir,' gasped Clarissa. 'Well, of all the cheek. This house is none of my brother's.'

'I think that between Charles and I we can endeavour to reconcile Lord Staines to the inevitability of Miss Thorne's residence here.'

Elfoy looked sceptical and Booth astonished, but he caught Grandiston's eye and so said, 'Oh, quite.'

It was some time later, on the drive home, before Charles was able to vent his feelings, 'How on earth are we to get

Staines to approve of Miss Thorne staying in a place that he has coveted for years? Not like you to give the ladies false hope, Hugo. Come to think of it, I'm not at all sure that your stratagems for fobbing off Thorne will work. If he hopes to profit from his sister's legacy, then a little local disapproval in Hertfordshire won't upset him.'

'The ladies require us to be knights-errant, Charles. They depend on us entirely. I'm sure that we can pull this off. The trick is to give everyone what they want.'

The Honourable Charles' handsome face took on an exasperated expression. 'Of course I mean to help the gels, that is, all the ladies of course, but I still don't see how ...'

Grandiston laid a hand on his shoulder in a placating fashion, 'What would be the least desirable thing for Staines in obtaining Ashcroft at the present?'

Charles looked blank then said, 'The cost, I'd say. An estate that size, even run down, would cost ...'

'Precisely Charles. You are not as dull-witted as I feared,' he ignored the young man's protest and continued, 'Now, supposing we could show Lord Staines a way to obtain the estate without the cost.' He paused and looked at his companion expectantly for a depressingly protracted period. Then:

'He could marry it!' shouted Charles brilliantly. Grandiston patted him on the shoulder. 'But I say, Hugo we can't really expect Miss Thorne to marry the fellow. It was only when we went to stay with him that I realized what a crashing bore he is – wouldn't foist him on that sweet girl for worlds. Strange that, you meet a fellow in the club and at the races, say, and he seems perfectly fine, then you go to a house party and discover he collects bird eggs or some such thing. You just never know old man.'

Grandiston grinned. 'Miss Thorne will not be expected to marry him, Charles, but Staines may at least be brought to *think* so.' Charles looked sceptical. 'Our stratagems are helped along by his vanity. He will, of course, believe that Miss Thorne must be overcome by his charms. We'll just put the thought in his Lordship's head. It is a delaying tactic. The longer the ladies remain at Ashcroft, the more difficult it will be for her brother to be seen to be acting in her best interests if he suggests their removal. The whole neighbourhood remarks the change in the estate. They are a remarkable group of women. I have yet another job for you, my dear boy.'

Charles looked suspicious, 'Yes?'

'It is time to enrich the neighbourhood further. If you were to go to the town, Charles, and let some of your acquaintance know the whereabouts of the beautiful Miss Petersham ...'

Chapter 11

Paying Calls

Mr Booth was not long delayed in town, but the ladies were busy in the meantime paying back all the calls from neighbours who had been denied their presence by the redoubtable Sullivan. Whilst Miss Micklethwaite kept to the house and estate, Misses Appleby, Petersham and Thorne drove the late viscount's landaulet around to make themselves known.

The first visit was to Lord Staines and his mother. Lord Grandiston happened to be visiting when the ladies were announced and began to see his plans take their first unexpected twist. As his lordship rose to greet Miss Thorne, the earl was pleased to see that his eyes lit up at the sight of such a pretty young heiress to the land he so cherished. The depth of his bow over Clarissa's outstretched hand was the sure sign of a beginning flirtation and Grandiston was pleased to think that his stratagems had worked so well. It did not last, however. As Staines rose, his eye alighted on her companion and his jaw dropped, as Clarissa noticed with amusement.

Oriana, who had given up her attempts to look like a school mistress since the appearance of her old friend, looked perfectly ravishing in a pale blue velvet pelisse and high crowned bonnet. The peacock feather that curled gently over the brim contained the deep green of her eyes whilst the golden curls framed a face so beautiful as to leave their host temporarily bereft of speech. Oh well, thought Grandiston - always a man to respond to the moment - that will do quite as well.

Lady Staines (in primrose and a pink shawl) took in the situation at a glance and came forward to welcome the ladies and to sit them down. 'Who is this girl?' she thought, 'Why didn't I catch her name?' However, Clarissa was introducing her and the silly Appleby woman again and her ladyship smiled easily while she thought madly. She had a natural bias against a young lady whose hair was the colour that she herself tried to maintain with great discomfort and who moreover had reduced her tiresome young son to a stuffed cabbage. When she heard her name though, she remembered the tales of Sir Fitzroy Petersham's sister who had been the season's beauty in a year when her own health had not permitted more than a short visit to town. Good birth then, but what was her fortune? She would send a letter to London tonight.

Lord Staines had at last recovered himself and addressed himself to Oriana.

'I am acquainted with your brother, Miss Petersham,' he said, with a warm glance.

Oriana's eyes burned fiery ice and she said indifferently, 'Oh, yes?'

Grandiston was diverted. Poor Staines. He could not have hit upon anything less winning to say to the object of his gallantry.

Clarissa interjected, momentarily drawing Staines' eyes away from the icy, but beautiful, Miss Petersham.

'I believe you are acquainted with my brother also, are you not sir?'

The Earl liked the little lady more and more - this was going for poor Staines' throat since the only occasion he had to meet her brother was when he had hoped to arrange the sale of Ashcroft without her own consent. But his Lordship recovered well, 'Yes, I had that pleasure whilst he was visiting the district on some business of yours, I believe.'

Clarissa could not help herself from replying, 'No business of mine, I assure you, my Lord.'

There was a brief pause before Lady Staines inquired archly, 'And how do you like the new tenants of the Dower House, my dear? Do you see much of Mr Booth?'

For some reason the natural response to this sounded a trifle off, for both young ladies realized that their tenant and his companion had been spending rather more time with them than was usual. Unexpectedly, Miss Appleby came quite smoothly to their rescue, 'Indeed we do. We ladies so enjoy the gentlemen's occasional visits for we found,' she leant forward confidingly towards her Ladyship, 'that Lord Grandiston here was Sir Ralph's dearest friend and an old friend of Miss Petersham's family. Was anything so fortunate? Of course the dear boys do get tired untangling our silks for us and the like. A houseful of women such as we are poor company for *London* men.' Here she smiled teasingly at Lord Grandiston who could not afterwards decide if she knew how masterfully respectable she made the gentlemen's visits seem.

Lord Staines thereafter tried to thaw out Miss Petersham with no success. Only for the shortest time of novelty had she enjoyed being accounted beautiful when she had gone to London. With little help from her brother she had soon tired of the fulsome compliments and disturbing attentions. Even the least silly of her suitors had seemed to wish to talk more about her beauty than her real self and she had become both bored and oppressed by it. Another suitor could not please her - especially not one who was friend to her despised brother.

The ladies took their leave and Grandiston walked them to the carriage. As he handed Oriana up he smiled at her. 'Strive to keep your temper in check, ice maiden. A little kindness from you may cause Lord Staines to be a little less interested in doing business so quickly with Mr Thorne.'

She looked disgusted, 'Grandiston, I could not be kind to that toad.'

She looked so much like her sixteen-year-old self that he gave a crack of laughter. 'Oriana, my dear, think of Clarissa,' he said caressingly.

The steps were up, Oriana's eyes flashed at him, they drove away and the earl laughed after them.

In the next days they visited old Sir Montague Holmes, the eldest and sweetest of the neighbourhood gentry whose bluff good humour had delighted them. He was unfortunately kept to his square manor house with bad health, but he invited the ladies to come again soon. He showed a strong disposition to flirt with Miss Appleby, which seemed to render her strangely quiet and shy instead of giddy as she had been in the presence of Booth and Grandiston. However, she did remember a family remedy which she hoped might allay the worst of Sir Montague's spasms and she offered to make it up and send it to him from Ashcroft. Sir Montague thanked her but fixed her with his rather bleary eyes and suggested, 'Why don't you bring it, my dear? I daresay I'd need advice on how to take it and so on.' Miss Appleby blushed and gave no promise.

The vicar and his wife and their pretty daughters Charlotte and Annabel welcomed them next and introduced the most prominent of the ladies of the village to their notice. Miss Petersham was attested to be the most beautiful of young ladies, but loyal to their district, the ladies were happy to see a real quality in Clarissa - a real look of the *old* viscount.

The most important call, in Clarissa's mind, was the one made to Mr Elfoy's mother.

This lady lived in a modest, but substantial stone cottage on the edge of the village with a garden as neatly tended as any they had seen. The fat thatch and the polished mullioned windows were a perfect prospect and the lady that came to meet them was a surprise. Her hair was perfectly white, but prematurely so, for a dignified and handsome face belied the white hair. She smiled a genuine welcome but Clarissa felt a little reserve in her which melted when she found that she was not to be treated to any patronage by the young ladies and melted still further as they both enthused about the many qualities of her beloved son.

Oriana was amused and a little worried to note the extreme interest betrayed in each other by her friend and Mrs Elfoy. Obviously, the lady had some inkling of her son's feelings and was concerned for him. Despite this, she could not but take to the shining Clarissa and her request for help in getting to know her neighbours and her interest in village life.

Later that week, the young ladies were found by the newly returned Mr Booth and his companion in the morning room, having recently ushered out Lord and Lady Staines.

'Miss Thorne, ladies. Glad to find you at home. Just returned from town and come to pay my respects at once,' said the Hon. Charles, very much at his ease.

Clarissa greeted him in the same manner; 'You are our third morning callers, gentlemen, so do not be surprised if our stock of light conversation has totally dried up. Whoever said it was dull in the country. Pray be seated.'

'Ah,' said Charles, wisely, 'but you are an object of curiosity. Don't give it a thought; you'll be old news in a week.'

'Well,' laughed Oriana, 'Just such a curiosity as Farmer Skipton's prize bull, Clarissa. Now we understand our neighbours' kind attentions.' Clarissa let out a whoop at Charles' crestfallen expression and Mrs Micklethwaite intervened.

'That is quite enough from all of you. Well, your Lordship, you see the village embraces Clarissa - how can this help our cause?' She turned to the earl who was lounging on the settle playing idly with his quizzing glass and watching the interplay with a smile.

'Yes.' said Oriana with spirit, 'And what did you mean when you said I should be kind to that weasel Staines? I have just had to endure a whole twenty minutes of his company and he barely acknowledged the other ladies.'

'Quite right, my dear,' said Miss Appleby looking up from her Berlin work, 'Hardly a word to any of us even when his mamma called him to attention. I do not think she liked him being quite so attentive to you. She spoke to me aside a little and asked about Sir Fitzroy and your fortune and so on ... although in the most delicate way imaginable, of course.'

'Silly woman,' said Miss Micklethwaite, 'What possesses her to wear that shade of pink at her age. If we are all to dance to your tune, Grandiston, at least give us your thoughts.'

'My thoughts are to help Miss Thorne retain her inheritance.'

'Well, you can dashed well do that without asking Miss Petersham to encourage a devilishly dull fellow like Staines,' said Mr Booth who was just beginning to realize that he'd spent two days in town increasing the number of his rivals for the beautiful Miss Petersham. He did it because Grandiston requested it and also because he had a fair notion that it would disoblige Sir Fitzroy to have half the town know his sister's whereabouts.

'You are right as always, Charles. The fair Miss Petersham's icy demeanour will be no bar to Staines' devotion. It will merely increase it. He is by far too conceited to accept defeat.'

'Well!' exclaimed Oriana, at a loss.

Grandiston's eyes glittered. 'You wish to know what strategy I employ. It is simple. I thought that rather than buy the property, Staines may like to marry it.' Miss Appleby gave a fluttering gasp at so direct a speech, but Clarissa was merely interested.

'You might guess that I will not marry him, my lord.'

'Of course I did. We are playing a delaying game. If Staines is not so keen to see you ladies depart the country, he will deprive your brother of the instant sale that he hoped to persuade you into. My best plans have failed me, but his pursuit of Oriana answers just as well. You have indulged in this round of visits so that you establish deeper into the community making any assertion that you might be friendless and in need of your brother's protection a redundant one. All that you are set to achieve on the estate, though admirable, will very well anger him since you have acted without reference to his judgement.'

'But it is nothing to do with him – and besides, he knows as little as I did at first about running such a place,' cried Clarissa, stung.

'Of course, but you can hardly expect him to agree to that. Gentlemen are always presumed to have a wiser head than young ladies. Do not interrupt.' Clarissa subsided sheepishly. 'We have to give him some reasons *not* to take you away. So, one, we have the scandal that would result in the neighbourhood if he were to take away the best landlord that the estate has known since your grandfather.'

Clarissa blushed, but Miss Micklethwaite muttered gloomily, 'That's not saying much by all accounts.' She was stilled by a mock-stern look from Grandiston.

'Two, we take away his quick sale, or at least delay it and third, well, this is a little delicate ...'

'Before you go on to three, Grandiston,' Clarissa interjected, unconsciously using the familiar form towards him, 'I don't like *one*. Why should my brother care about upsetting this neighbourhood? He lives so far away, doesn't he?'

'Indeed, that is true. However, he travels to Bath and London, doesn't he? Doesn't his wife aspire to the *ton*? Well, the neighbourhood, unless I am much mistaken, is about to swell with London smarts who might very well disapprove of your removal from the estate.'

'Oh,' said Miss Appleby, interestedly, 'is there a sporting event in the area?'

'After a fashion,' said Grandiston wryly, 'I see that it is time for Charles to tell you what he was doing in town. Charles?' He raised his eyebrow quizzically in his friend's direction.

Mr Booth tugged awkwardly at his neckcloth and looked at the expectant ladies one by one, finally gulping as his frightened eye alighted on Oriana. 'I was only doing Grandiston's bidding, mind,' he said apologetically. 'Well, I was informing a few particular friends of the whereabouts of Miss Petersham,' he finished at a rush.

Sparing only a disgusted look at Booth, Oriana turned her green-eyed glare on the true culprit. 'Grandiston, you wretch,' she said, fuming; 'We'll have a hoard of men besieging this place.' She stopped flushing as she realized that she had been betrayed into unmaidenly speech.

Grandiston's eyes danced, 'Well I'm glad you are not falsely modest about your charms my dear.'

'I for one never doubted that your season was more successful than we knew, Oriana,' declared Clarissa in her friend's defence.

'Not my charms, as Grandiston realizes, but my inheritance,' said Oriana, contemptuously.

The ladies looked stunned. Little Miss Appleby looked to the earl for guidance, 'But Oriana, the dear girl, she is like all of us, without portion. Or else why would she have been at the academy?'

Oriana had composed herself with difficulty, grasping at her hands to keep her temper. 'It is well known in town that I have my mother's portion, which is considerable, when I reach the age of 25. My father was my mother's executor and it simply passed on to my brother when he died. The knowledge of my fortune made me much sought after, I assure you.'

Charles was moved to protest, 'I don't think that you'd need any fortune to get the attention,' he said frankly, 'why with a fig-,' he broke off in disarray, 'I mean ....'

'Yes, Mr Booth,' said Clarissa, amused, 'it is a lovely figure and quite the most beautiful face I have seen. What could make you think them after your money?'

Oriana turned towards her, giving a visible shudder as she did so. 'If you could have seen some of the men that my brother encouraged as my suitors. I had to endure morning visits from the most ...' Her eyes lowered and Grandiston began to see what her life in London had been like. Compelled by the manners of the day to politeness to anyone of whom her brother approved. His eyes narrowed in a way that did not bode well for the absent baronet.

'Now that the subject has been raised my dear Oriana, I have never been able to understand how your father – excellent man that he seems to have been - failed to provide for you himself,' said the timid little lady, displaying an uncharacteristic lack of delicacy.

'He didn't expect to fall off that horse,' declared Oriana.

'Unfortunate.' 'Careless.' 'Men.' declared Grandiston, Booth and Miss Micklethwaite in unison.

The company again descended to mirth and Oriana's passion found itself spent. Mr Booth declared himself still curious as to how an heiress had ended up a schoolteacher.

Grandiston leaned negligently on the high mantelpiece, 'Oh, I think we can hazard a guess can we not? Miss Petersham does not inherit for four years yet. Until then, it is either dance to her brother's tune or accept the protection of marriage. Having almost brought herself to the second option,' Oriana gasped and began to speak, but stopped with her face set in hard and haughty lines, 'she found she could not. With her habit of ordering her home for her father, I fear obeying such a brother as Sir Fitzroy would prove a task beyond her.'

'Can't blame her.' He looked guiltily at Oriana, 'Don't want to offend, Miss Petersham, but your brother is a dashed ... dashed ... ladies present.'

'Quite right, dreadful man,' approved Clarissa, 'I feel we are all such friends that we need not fear cutting up characters together comfortably. But, Lord Grandiston, I fear you are mistaken ...' she continued with her usual impetuosity but stopped as she encountered a look of passionate prohibition from Oriana's fine eyes, '... in thinking she is of a disobedient nature,' she finished lamely. Why should Oriana wish the earl to continue to believe that she had ever consented to that awful engagement? But so, it seemed, she did.

'If I am to be obedient, let me know what possible good this will do Clarissa,' fumed Oriana, turning towards Grandiston.

He laughed, 'Well, it will increase the gentry of the neighbourhood - making it more difficult for her brother to take a high hand, more likely that he will wish to increase his acquaintance, if as you say Clarissa, he hankers after rank.' He strode forward and raised Oriana's chin with his finger. 'What's the matter, Pigeon, is your friendship so easily tested?' He caught her eyes in his, his voice teasing.

His hand on her, so intimately as of yore, sent the flames into her blood, her heart racing. He'd used his childhood name for her and for some reason she could not fathom, it wounded her to the heart. It caused her to pull away from him and say in a thickened voice, 'I love you dearly, Clarissa, but why is it I who have to suffer first Staines' and then who knows whose attentions?'

Grandiston turned suavely away to lean nonchalantly against the mantle. 'But that is where you are wrong, my dear, Clarissa too must suffer some attentions for our plan to work.'

'Won't work,' said Clarissa bluntly, 'Staines is smitten already. I daresay I couldn't get him to notice me even if I borrowed one of his mother's frightful hats.'

'My dears, there is a lack of delicacy in this conversation that I must ...' said Miss Appleby faintly, with a fluttering protest of her lace handkerchief.

'Later, Louisa,' interrupted Miss Micklethwaite. She turned to Grandiston. 'I fancy you don't mean Staines, sir, do you?'

Grandiston bowed his head towards her, the eyes still dancing. 'Your intelligence never disappoints me, ma'am. Given her brother's predilection for rank, I believe the attentions of, say, an earl to his sister might impress him, don't you?'

Charles gave a crack of laughter and Clarissa plopped suddenly onto the sofa, her hand at her breast in shock.

Grandiston bowed mockingly and said, 'what do you say, Clarissa?'

In a coy manner, reminiscent of Miss Appleby's finest, Clarissa held out her hand and turned her head away. 'What can I say, my lord?' she simpered, 'except - this is so sudden.'

Miss Appleby looked confused, but the rest laughed and it was so ridiculous that even Oriana joined in. Why, though, did she feel an icicle steal into her heart? Grandiston was bowing graciously over her hand and the tableau, though obviously staged, arrested her. Her young friend was so fascinating these days, she might very well capture his heart truly - why should she care so much?

Sullivan entered, uttering, 'Mr Elfoy and Miss Sowersby, ma'am.'

Grandiston dropped Clarissa's hand but not before Mr Elfoy had taken in the picture with horror. He brought up short and Grandiston, turning towards the door, was amused but not surprised to encounter a look from young Elfoy's eye that would have been fatal, if looks could kill.

Clarissa, all unawares, dashed past him to embrace his companion, an exquisitely turned out young lady wearing a turquoise pelisse over her travelling dress and a hat that could only have come from London, trimmed in the same coloured velvet ribbons.

'Juliana!' exclaimed Clarissa and encompassed her in a warm hug.

CHAPTER 12

Juliana Arrives

Juliana Sowersby received her friend's embrace warmly then looked shyly at the assembled company. She was a slender girl with pale blonde hair and a rather gentle face, which might have been pretty but for the look of alarm on her face at the sight of the Earl of Grandiston.

Her mamma had decided that a great marriage was for her and had rather thrown Juliana at the eligible earl's head at one ball and another supper party that they had both attended in London. Juliana, overwhelmed by so prestigious a presence, had found herself completely tongue-tied in his company. His high, dismissive manner had shrivelled her spirits for some time.

Clarissa was mouthing introductions and she shook hands as best she could, but she was feeling a little low from the journey and from the stifling presence of the earl whom she none the less greeted with her shy good manners. She began to feel a little faint when she gratefully heard the stout blunt lady, Miss Mickle-something, say to Clarissa, 'I think that your friend should rest after her journey, Clarissa. Why don't you take her upstairs?'

'Indeed,' said her friend guiltily, 'Come with me. I must see you to your chamber. I never dreamed you would be able to come so quickly. Thank you, Mr Elfoy, for ushering her in. Should you object to waiting for an hour before we discuss the building work? Or stay for dinner ...' she placed a hand on his arm as she passed him and only waited for the slight bow of his head in agreement. His arm burned through his jacket and he was afraid that a faint flush might give away his feelings to the company. Little did he know that everyone, excepting only Mr Booth and Miss Appleby, had been aware of his feelings for weeks.

Miss Appleby ushered the gentlemen out saying, 'Yes, you must all come to dinner to welcome our guest. It is so fortunate that we ordered the lamb dressed for tonight. I must go down and tell cook that there are four more for dinner.'

Miss Micklethwaite sat down with her needlework, sighing at the small oasis of peace at last when a thought struck her that caused her to tug the ancient bell-pull by the mantle. The butler made a stately entrance.

'Sullivan, it may be that some young gentlemen may pay us a visit this afternoon.'

'Yes, miss. Their names?'

'Lord, how should I know? Acquaintances of Miss Petersham from *London*' she said the word with disdain. 'Deny us until tomorrow.'

'Certainly Ma'am' said the Imperturbable, closing the door softly behind him.

Miss Micklethwaite allowed herself to lean against the chair back and omit another satisfied sigh before picking up her work again.

Meanwhile, Juliana had removed her pelisse and hat, both of which Clarissa exclaimed over, and was now sitting holding hands with Clarissa and telling her about her season in London. She talked of the balls, the parties and the great rush of people on the streets, all so new to her, and how kind everyone had been. Clarissa caught the exhausted look in her eye and said, 'But you didn't like it, did you dear Juliana?'

Juliana was not of an over-confiding nature but her spirits were so low that she burst into tears at these words and cast herself on Clarissa's bosom. In broken sentences and convoluted narrative she poured out her story. Although she had enjoyed her first London season, it had been full of the fear of meeting new and sophisticated people. She could have got over that if she had not known that it was her mother's dearest wish to have her engaged by the end of it. Her mother loved her but she was as impervious as Juliana was sensitive. She was not subtle in her manner of fostering alliances and her overt behaviour made Juliana a gibbering wreck. Her mother had gently reprimanded her on showing a want of spirit in the enterprise and she was consequently miserable. When Clarissa's letter came, it was her kind father who had taken her face between his hands and adjured her to go and stay with her friend until her mother had recovered her spirits.

'I was so sorry to disoblige her, but I did not meet anyone I could be comfortable with in the least,' she ended in a rush.

'I'm sure your mama would not wish you to be unhappy, Juliana,' said Clarissa comfortingly.

Juliana smiled and brushed at her tears, 'Oh, I know. It's perfectly foolish of me, I feel better now. But tell me about you. Your hair is different; you look so happy, Clarissa. Tell me everything.'

'Well yes I will,' said Clarissa, 'But first you must know that I've brought you here to join a conspiracy.' Then she poured out her tale of her brother's imminent arrival and some of the measures they had taken to make it difficult for him to order her home. She saw that Juliana was more amused than shocked at her behaviour, but she still left out Grandiston's plot to pay court to her. She did not think it would be so easy to explain this to her well brought up friend.

Juliana listened with great admiration to her friend. How could Clarissa be so bold as to take all this upon herself? She could only be in awe of her determination and resolve. If only she had such courage, but even knowing Clarissa's brother she feared that she herself would have taken the easy way out. She said as much to her friend and Clarissa laughed merrily, her eyes twinkling mischievously, 'You wrong yourself, dear Juliana, else you would now be engaged to some suitor of your mother's choosing.'

Juliana was much struck by this. 'You are quite right,' she said, astonished, 'Oh, how glad I am to have come to see you, Clarissa, you *always* contrive to make me feel good about myself.'

So it was at dinner that evening that Juliana was not as overwhelmed by the earl's presence as she had expected to be. He seemed to be in a permanently mellow mood, quite unlike his London manners. Oriana, Clarissa, Mr Elfoy and he seemed to be talking animatedly about the refurbishment of the estate houses and crop rotations. Mr Booth was gently flirting with Miss Appleby and teasing Miss Micklethwaite who treated him rather like a naughty schoolboy. Juliana felt shy amongst the intimacy of the company but realised that little was expected of her. Her shawl fell from her shoulders and Mr Booth retrieved it with a friendly smile. How kind he was and how handsome. Yet he did not seem to terrify her as other young men had done.

The Honourable Charles, meanwhile, was feeling a little for the young lady. The others were so busy that they did not seem to notice her shyness, so he resolved to make her feel more the thing. What a dear little smile she had given him when he had passed a platter to her. She didn't seem to have enjoyed London much when she replied to Miss Micklethwaite's inquiries. It seemed to him that her parents had not taken enough care of her. Of course she'd be shy, a young girl like that, she needed a little help to feel more at ease. Charming too, thought Charles, not a beauty like the divine Miss Petersham or vivacious like Miss Thorne, but she had a soft gentle face that he liked.

He had meant to pay a more resolute court to Oriana after dinner; but he found himself instead setting a chair by the fire for the new arrival, disposing her shawl for her, and offering to turn her pages for her when she consented to play the pianoforte. This turned out to be a further icebreaker between her and the company, for the tuning of the piano was a task hitherto forgotten in the overhaul of the house. Nervously playing her nocturne, Juliana had soon to join in the gales of laughter at the truly dreadful sound she was producing. She stopped, but Clarissa burst out, 'Oh, keep playing, do. I have not been so diverted for ages.' She played on jauntily and said when she finished, 'I wish I might borrow your instrument, Clarissa. I do not know when my playing has pleased so much.'

At that precise moment, the butler ushered in a visitor.

'Mr Thorne, ma'am.'

Clarissa stopped laughing and stood up, the blood draining from her face. Oriana went to her side and gripped her hand tightly.

John Thorne came in still bundled up in his travelling coat with the capes at the shoulders and his buckskin and breeches. He was taken aback to see so many people in the room, especially gentlemen, and outrage rose in his chest, already begun by seeing the changes to the gardens and the house which he had witnessed driving up. He was cold and miserable but nevertheless had come prepared to forgive his erring sister whom he expected to be regretting her foolhardy behaviour. Now he saw her at the centre of the room looking prettier than he had ever seen her, with her hair clustering in curls around her face. Her dress was black as befitted her mourning, but of a cut and quality that he had never seen adorn her. For the evening, she had left off her fichu and her gown showed her figure to a flattering extent. Why it should enrage him to see her thus he did not examine, he just uttered in an outraged tone, 'Clarissa.'

Miss Micklethwaite's even, blunt tones interrupted him. 'Good evening, John.' she said, 'I do hope you've cleaned your boots; the carpet is Chinese, you know.'

Stopped dead by the guilt that only a childhood voice of authority can produce, Mr Thorne looked at his feet for a second before his dignity reasserted itself, 'Good evening, Miss Micklethwaite. Miss Appleby,' he said politely, then turned to his sister, 'I did not expect to find you hosting a *party,* Clarissa. It is not right.'

Mr Elfoy felt his hackles rise. The fire that was in him wished to have the right to avenge that tone of voice being used against Clarissa. He so far forgot himself as to step forward but was restrained by a strong hand. Grandiston watched as Clarissa, at first confounded by her brother's appearance, pulled herself valiantly forward. Pure pluck that girl. The whole company knew that the young prig of a brother could order her home with him this instant and there was little to be done about it, yet she was keeping her head and sticking to her plan. She moved forwards and extended her hands.

'John!' she cried, 'How nice to see you,' he was obliged to take her hands and follow as she ushered him into the room, chatting as she went. 'Hardly a party, John. I am still in mourning for my cousin the viscount as you see.'

'What I see, Clarissa,' he hissed beneath his breath, 'is beyond ...'

'You must let me introduce you to everyone,' blithely continued his sister, 'You remember Mr Elfoy from your visit here?'

John became as ramrod stiff with politeness as his slightly portly frame would allow, and he bowed an inch. Mr Elfoy, following Clarissa's lead, bowed back politely, his face masking his anxious desire to plant his fist in Mr Thorne's face. 'Mr Elfoy kindly joined us this evening to discuss estate business.'

John could not let this pass.

'I should think, my dear Clarissa, that you should rather leave business to gentlemen.'

'I'm sure you are right, John,' she said untruthfully, then swept on, 'You know Miss Petersham, of course.' John stared in disbelief at Oriana, whom he had last seen in the schoolroom wearing brown calico, resplendent tonight in a cream silk gown and spangled shawl that had cost her father a hundred guineas in Paris. He nodded, bemused. 'And I have a surprise for you, John, an old acquaintance.'

Juliana, who had been sitting behind the piano, stood up. 'Mr Thorne - how nice to see you again. I hope all is well with dearest Mrs Thorne and the children?'

'Miss Sowersby!' he exclaimed. '*You* here.' John felt that he was dreaming. Nothing was as he expected it, especially not to see the daughter of the first family of his home district so comfortably ensconced in his sister's drawing room. The last thing he could afford to do was to upset her.

Juliana had not been requested to do much but be here, but John Thorne's tone to Clarissa had offended her so she took advantage of his confusion.

'I hope you are not deceived as to the nature of our little dinner. Having just arrived on ... on an *extended* visit to my dearest Miss Thorne, I discovered that her Dower House tenants were ... were friends of mine from London. How kind of your sister to invite them to dinner, for my sake.'

Mr Booth gave a crack of laughter, which he disguised as a cough. He caught Juliana's eye and gave her an admiring look that made her blush, then held out his hand to Thorne, 'My name's Booth.' John shook his hand whilst casting a glance at Clarissa and muttering, '*Tenants.*'

'So sorry.' continued Clarissa, beginning to enjoy herself, 'The Honourable Charles Booth, my tenant, and his companion, The Earl of Grandiston.'

Miss Appleby shook her head distractedly. Oh dear, when *would* Clarissa learn that etiquette decreed that Grandiston should have been introduced first? she thought. She continued to observe the introductions with little understanding of the subtleties of the reactions around her.

Mr Thorne was completely overawed by the elegant figure of the earl and bowed low. Grandiston looked bored and became again, as Juliana watched him, the very picture of languid indifference that she had met and feared in London. As John murmured about the honour of meeting him, Grandiston met Juliana's eye over his head and she thought she discerned a twinkle in his eyes that caused her to feel comfortable again.

Miss Micklethwaite lifted her considerable bulk from the chair and bustled forward. 'The gentlemen were just leaving, John. I am sure that you can make their acquaintance again.'

Mr Thorne was confused and stood back as the earl bowed to the ladies and then stopped at Clarissa and took her hand, bending over it. Clarissa was betrayed into a giggle, but her brother did not see because Grandiston pinched her sharply.

Thorne's eyes widened as he took in the earl's smile at Clarissa. A thought struck him - could the earl be interested in *his* sister? An earl in the family. Not just aristocracy, but one of the highest ranking noblemen in the land. And one of the richest.

CHAPTER 13

Mr Thorne's Intentions

It seemed John Thorne was to have no more conversation with his sister that evening. Juliana feigned a headache and Clarissa led her from the room, requiring Miss Appleby to see to his needs. This she did in her usual manner, talking as she went.

'My dear boy, you must be so tired. What a long journey. Yes, I know you wish to speak to Clarissa but she cannot well leave her guest. You would not like her to complain to her mamma about her treatment here, would you? Mm? The house is much improved since we arrived; this staircase was so dirty that it cannot have been cleaned for years, I daresay. You will be so proud of the improvements your sister has made - oh, I forgot, you have visited here before us haven't you? No doubt you saw how they have tamed those trees along the driveway? NO? Well, it was dark, I suppose. I have ordered a hot brick but would you like some chocolate before bed? I remember that you used to prefer it when you were younger ...'

Mr Thorne was eventually settled in the Chinese bedroom and persuaded her that he was comfortable enough. This was not comfort- it was luxury. The finest linen was on the bed, and a silk coverlet matched the bed hangings. He had to remember that this was his sister's house now. When last he had seen it, he had recognized its beauty, but the air of disuse and neglect had made it unappealing. Now the floors gleamed and the ancient furniture shone. He preferred his own cosy room with Cornelia in it, but still he could not but be impressed. However, these plans were going too far. Clarissa must be brought to heel soon. The sooner the house was sold the better. Tenants in the Dower House. That could hold things up. He must check with Elfoy how long their lease is. And yet, an earl. If only Cornelia were here. She would so enjoy telling the neighbourhood of her meeting with a member of the *haut ton,* the very ruler of fashion.

He got out of bed and wrote his wife a letter on the notepaper still emblazoned by the late viscount's coat of arms.

Ushered into the breakfast room the next morning, he was lucky enough to find his sister alone.

'Well Clarissa. Things have changed here indeed. I suppose you must be very pleased with yourself.'

Words came readily to Clarissa's mouth but she swallowed them down with sip of chocolate before she found a more diplomatic reply, 'I am lucky that Mr Elfoy takes such good care of things,' she said meekly.

John's eyes narrowed a little as he searched her eyes for signs of irony: meek was not usually a tone he associated with Clarissa. She gave him back a frank gaze, however, and added, 'For the rest, it is just good housekeeping ... and Waity organizes us like Wellington.'

John gave a short laugh, 'That I can well believe.' He walked around the room like an admiral on inspection, nodding at the gleaming sideboards and the silver candlesticks with approval, 'Well, well. You have done the old place proud. It should fetch a much better price in good order.'

Clarissa's spoon clattered in her saucer but her eyes remained lowered and her hands trembled a little as she raised her cup to her mouth. She could not trust herself to speak.

'I was most displeased to find you gone from the school. I daresay you did not realize it, but I had already begun to deal with the burden of your inheritance for you. It is my wish that you make your home with me and I am charged by Cornelia to tell you of the welcome that awaits you.'

'That is very kind of Cornelia,' said Clarissa brightly, remembering in detail how 'welcome' she had been made to feel on her last visit to her brother's house, 'However, I would prefer to remain here for the present.'

John's voice took on a steely tone, 'What you would *prefer*, Clarissa, is not what is at issue. You cannot remain here alone and though you have done a great deal to improve the look of Ashcroft you can have no notion what it takes to run a great estate. You have neither the money nor the expertise to do so. You might be ruined within the year.' Clarissa's hand gripped her damask napkin as though it were a lifeline. 'I did mean us to journey back this day but your foolhardy agreement to rent the Dower House has put me in a difficult position. I shall have to stay a little and see what may be contrived about the lease. I'll talk to Elfoy today.'

His assumption of rights was almost all that Clarissa could stand, in spite of her promising Waity and Oriana to do nothing to annoy her brother. She was saved from an outburst by the entrance of the rest of the ladies but the look she flashed at Miss Micklethwaite was enough to put that lady in the picture.

'Sit up straight John, do.' she told him after the morning greetings had been exchanged, 'you always were given to slouching.' Clarissa shot her another look, this time of pure gratitude as she saw John collapse promptly from the pompous older brother to erring schoolboy.

She soon escaped with Juliana and Oriana to change for their ride in the park whilst John was detained by Miss Micklethwaite and Miss Appleby's requests for news of his family. As they were about to set out with Mr Elfoy, that gentleman was detained by Mr Thorne.

'I wish to speak to you, sir.'

'Certainly,' replied Tristram, politely. If his respectful tone was ironic, Mr Thorne didn't notice.

'It is about the Dower House lease.'

Mr Elfoy mounted his horse, and said, 'Then it had better wait until later, sir, since you must know that I am not at liberty to speak of estate matters without the permission of my mistress.' As he touched his hat in salute and swung the horse forward to join the ladies, Mr Thorne was left fulminating on the steps.

Up the Dower House path, the Earl of Grandiston and The Honourable Mr Booth were riding towards him. Thorne stood up straighter and arranged his face into a greeting.

'My lord, Mr Booth. Good morning.'

'Mr Thorne - charmed to see you once more. Is Miss Thorne ready for her morning ride yet? We thought we might join her this fine morning,' said the Earl smoothly.

'Oh my Lord, I'm sorry,' said Thorne obsequiously, 'They have left. Would you care to step inside for – for ...' his imagination gave way, 'a rest?'

'No, indeed sir,' said Charles, 'We'll catch up ...' He stopped as Grandiston's whip made sharp contact with his knee.

'How kind, Mr Thorne,' said the earl, 'we'd be delighted, eh Charles?' He had already dismounted and had clasped an arm around John's shoulder saying, 'Call me Grandiston.'

Clarissa, meanwhile, was enjoying a vent to her feelings by telling Mr Elfoy and her friends of her brother's perfidy. Juliana was surprised that Mr Elfoy was party to her confidences, but was now rolling with the surprises. Never before had she been part of such a strange tangle of relations, but she was becoming used to it.

'*Then* he said that what I *preferred* was not at issue,' Clarissa was saying, her faced flushed with indignation, 'I declare he is as much a tyrant as ... as ... Napoleon. Just marching in here trying to conquer yet more territory. Well I shall not have it. How I contrived to keep from throwing the marmalade at him, I cannot conceive.'

Juliana giggled. 'You are so brave. I cannot bear it when gentlemen raise their voices.'

'Keeping your nerve is all you can do for the moment, my dear. You know that Grandiston has us all in hand. I believe that he will know how to proceed, though I'm loath to admit it. He's the most highhanded ....' said Oriana, reaching over her saddle to grasp her friend's hand.

Mr Elfoy coughed and raised a humorous eyebrow. 'Well, yes. I couldn't help noticing that the company you are keeping impressed your brother.'

'Yes, and though he was angry about the Dower House tenancy, he has delayed our departure, probably with the purpose of furthering Grandiston's acquaintance,' she giggled, 'Just to think, Cornelia's missing a real live earl. She'll never forgive him.'

'Oh yes,' said Juliana, 'but Mr Elfoy, surely Mr Thorne cannot force Clarissa to sell up?'

Tristram looked around at the ladies ruefully, 'Well, he cannot, of course. However, she is young enough that he could be considered her guardian and oblige her to live with him.' He frowned, 'If that were to happen, it would be the worse for the tenants, I think. He might forbid correspondence and then the estate would go back to the state that you found it and worse.'

Clarissa looked grave. 'I would be *obliged* to sell.'

'Clarissa!' said Oriana.

'Any landlord is better than one who cannot manage. There are the tenants to think of,' she replied, glumly.

Oriana's head went up and her beautiful green eyes flashed fire.

'We will trust to Grandiston.' Then her voice changed as she said, 'Oh, *no*.'

Clarissa saw with amusement what had made her cry out. Riding towards them down the long avenue were three young exquisites dressed for the country as only London tailors know how to achieve. One sported a striped waistcoat and spotted necktie that conveyed to London Misses Petersham and Sowersby the unmistakable raiment of the Four Horse Club, but made Clarissa and Tristram, unacquainted with the eccentric attire sported by these young blades, share an unholy grin. The second gentleman wore a very dashing, if rather impractical tall hat whose sheen was only secondary to the sheen of his splendid, gold-tasselled topboots. The third man dressed in a quieter manner, yet his elegance superseded his companions. He was certainly the handsomest man Clarissa had ever seen (excepting perhaps one), with dark wavy hair curling rakishly over his startling eyes. He smiled meltingly at Oriana as the others hailed her.

'Miss Petersham,' began the first, 'Well met.'

Clarissa was amused to see that the little line between Oriana's eyebrows meant that she did not agree with this sentiment, but she bowed her head civilly enough and concocted a smile, 'Sir Piers, how do you do? What brings you to Ashcroft?'

'Why, only the hint that you might be found here, Miss Petersham,' said Sir Piers Loxley frankly.

'And Lord Russell?' the second gentleman took his hat from his head (to the detriment of his carefully arranged hair) as he sketched a bow from horseback. 'Miss Petersham,' he breathed, 'the absence of Aphrodite from London has cast us all adrift.' Clarissa could not help smiling as Oriana's face froze into distaste at this compliment, but she just touched his proffered hand,

'Monsieur le Duc de Montaigne.' Her voice temperature lowered and she inclined her head only slightly to the third gentleman.

'Mademoiselle. I am charmed as ever,' murmured the Duc, with the slightest of French accents.

She introduced her companions as form suggested, but did not seek to detain the visitors longer. Clarissa, mindful of Grandiston's instructions and ignoring Oriana's sigh, invited the gentlemen to the house for refreshments before they rode back to the village.

This was only the first of the calls that were made on the ladies. Throughout, Oriana sat in magnificent disdain whilst the variety of gentlemen endeavoured to engage her in conversation. Clarissa thought that perhaps a little friendliness might have caused some gentlemen to find her less fascinating, though there didn't seem any way to tell her friend this. She was a beautiful mystery, a challenge, and her behaviour simply made her more unattainable and therefore more desirable.

Still, the house seemed full of people all of a sudden, although Sullivan rationed the visits by the young gentlemen.

The Dower House tenants had begun to wander in through the French windows without any ceremony encouraged by Mr Thorne, who was beginning to think of himself as an intimate of the aristocracy. He was, moreover, bowled over by Oriana's other suitors, even though an impoverished French Dukedom could not rival an English Earl, the foreigner's sleek charm impressed him. A baronet like Sir Piers (someone he would have felt honoured to meet normally) was almost beneath his notice in this exalted company until Charles whispered in his ear that he was rich as Croesus - worth thirty thousand a year. John's head was turned. The hint of the attention that Grandiston was paying to Clarissa silenced any complaint about his extended stay from Cornelia. Indeed, only a visit from her mother was detaining her from visiting Ashcroft herself. For which Clarissa would have been very grateful had she known.

Clarissa, too, found herself courted and was mightily entertained. Sir Piers at least seemed to prefer her vivacity to her friend's coldness and flattered her outrageously. She had never had such attention and had not been used to thinking of herself as pretty. Perhaps it was the inheritance, she thought, but there was no sense in pretending that the company of young highly spirited men was not a diversion from her worries.

In fact, she looked so charming and had such vivacity that Oriana's beaux (whilst most remained devoted) were captivated. Such was the behaviour of Sir Piers that anyone would have assumed he had now come to woo Clarissa. Mr Thorne had an excellent opportunity to see how well his sister's chaperones shielded her from an excess of attention.

Mr Elfoy more than once had met them riding in the park, once with Sir Piers adjusting Clarissa's hands on the reins to instruct her in getting the feel of a difficult horse. Clarissa had been laughing up at him and Tristram had ridden his horse in the opposite direction at the gallop. He did not even have the release of disliking the baronet - he was a very good sort of fellow. It must be a comfort to him that Clarissa was being courted by gentlemen who might offer her protection from her brother.

M. Le Duc, though, kept his fulminating black eyes on Oriana.

Juliana meanwhile felt shy but much more at her ease than in London. No one expected her to shine in conversation and she had not the leading remarks of her matchmaking (but very loving) mama to put her to the blush. Whenever the banter left her out a little, she would soon find Mr Booth at her side; talking to her in the easiest way, fetching her shawl if she was a little chilly and listening to her tell tales (that must have bored him, she thought) about her parents and her beloved home.

It was after about two weeks of going along in this way that Grandiston, Booth and Thorne joined the ladies in a walk after luncheon, as usual. Juliana fell behind a little, as she had to stoop and take a stone from her slipper. She was sitting on a tree stump replacing it when Charles came back for her.

'Are you quite well, Miss Sowersby?' said Charles in his bluff way; 'Can I help?'

Juliana blushed and covered her ankles quickly, 'No, indeed, sir,' she said, 'Just a tiresome pebble. I am quite ready to set off again.'

The others were ahead of them, in plain sight. Mr Thorne was boring Oriana whilst Grandiston entertained Clarissa. They did not rush to join them but ambled on companionably together. Charles looked a little troubled and when Juliana mentioned it, he found himself telling her of a letter from his father sardonically applauding his conversion to country life and reminding him that he was heir to an estate quite as rural as his present address. Soon, with a little gentle prodding, he found himself confiding to her the long standing resentment and guilt that characterized their relationship. Finally, sitting on a style, he admitted, 'He thinks I'm a fool, of course. And why shouldn't he? I've behaved like one so often. I'm not the son he hoped for.'

He looked so much like a lost boy, with his hair shaggily hanging over his bowed head that Juliana touched his arm with one little kid gloved hand. 'Oh no,' she said softly and simply, 'How could that be? I expect you are very alike and he loves you just as much as I can see that you love him.'

Charles gazed down at her gentle grey eyes as she spoke to him and fell into them headlong. She was very different from any girl he had ever known. Her shyness did not conceal silliness like so many others, just a soft yielding nature and a kindness that he had noted again and again. At first he had simply been aware of the protective instinct she aroused in him to fill in for her inability to put herself forward. She was pretty in a quieter way than Oriana's beauty or Clarissa's expressive face but when she smiled as she did now, she stopped his heart.

'Oh, Juliana,' he breathed, drawing her into his arms. She fell into them yieldingly and their lips met with a trembling promise of the fire that had sprung between them.

As she pulled away, Juliana breathed, 'Oriana. Don't you love her?'

Charles chuckled, his arms still about her waist, 'Apparently not,' he said ruefully, 'like every other man in London,

I thought I did. The lovely Miss Petersham has never cared a button for me. Nor I for her, now I know what love is. It's so ... so comfortable isn't it?' His eyes were grave for a second, unsure whether she really understood but she nodded, her eyes shining into his. 'When can I speak to your father, my love?'

Juliana recalled herself to sense. 'Let me go Mr Booth ... Charles ... we must catch up with the others.'

With glad hearts they resumed their walk. Whatever Juliana said to the contrary, Charles was determined to begin his travels to her parents' home that day to ask her father for his daughter's hand. 'I shouldn't have kissed you till it's settled, old girl. So I shall make amends by leaving as quickly as possible.'

Juliana was a little concerned that Mr Booth, whilst heir to a tidy estate and a respectable title was not the great prospect that her mother had schemed for: but when she looked at Charles she was too much in love to suppose that they could fail to be overwhelmed by his magnificence.

The air of joy was too palpable to be ignored by any but the self-centred Mr Thorne. Later, in Juliana's bedroom, all could be told in heart-wrenching detail to the whoops of delight of the young ladies.

'Well,' remarked Clarissa eventually, 'Whilst Oriana and I have been doing all the talking in the morning room, it is you that has been getting her man. How sly.'

Juliana threw her pillow at her.

CHAPTER 14

Oriana in Trouble

Clarissa and Oriana were overjoyed by the good news of their friend, but they both had their own problems to face.

Clarissa was becoming more and more exasperated with her brother's presence and she was feeling a certain invisible curtain between her and her Miss Petersham.

Oriana's spirits, on the other hand, were becoming abraded by the repeated visits of her beaux. A few of the more out and out fortune hunters had driven from London only to be sent on their way by the redoubtable Miss Micklethwaite and her henchman, Sullivan, but still more arrived and had to be admitted on the grounds of good manners. Many were acquaintances from London or self-declared friends of her father. To suffer the gentle flattery (nothing too outrageous might be said in front of her chaperones) was bad enough, but occasionally she had to suffer it under the sardonic eye of Grandiston. He came to pay punctilious court to Clarissa within the beaming gaze of Mr Thorne, and even though Oriana knew the game in this, she could not but be lowered by the sight of her friends enjoying each other's company. For whatever they were doing, Oriana could see that Clarissa really made his eyes light up with laughter, just as they had used to smile on her.

She could not draw him to her because she was still very angry with him. How *could* he think she had become engaged in that dreadfully self-serving way and then been unable to go through with it? He did not know her at all if that is what he thought. So she smiled and was passably friendly to him but she kept herself from him, though she longed to roam the grounds, ride, jest and fight with him as she had in the old days.

After a dreadful set of morning visits yesterday, when Staines had brought his chair oppressively close to her and tried to engage her in conversation about her odious brother whilst Grandiston met her eyes with a gleam in his that only made her more furious, she decided that she would avoid the visits today. To that end she escaped the house in her riding dress and sent a boy to have her horse brought around to the side entrance.

As luck would have it, M. le Duc de Montaigne was riding from that direction and could see her standing in her pale blue velvet habit as her horse arrived. She mounted her horse as he rode up.

'Ah, Mademoiselle, I am so happy to meet you at your exercise. May I not join you?'

Oriana was annoyed but there seemed to be nothing for it but to agree. She did not trust the Duc, but he was a man of more address than his fellows and he had known better than to press his suit too strongly. As they rode off together he began to talk of their London acquaintance in so unexceptional a way that she began to relax. Her withered nerves began to sooth and she even laughed at his tale of Lord Sutcliffe's creaking corset at the last soiree at Almack's.

'Ah, you are so lovely when you smile,' he said, his accent thickening and his eyes smouldering.

It was a mistake. Oriana lost her smile and gave thanks that they had not gone too far from the house.

'I believe I shall canter before returning. I am rather tired.'

He quickened his pace along with her, but then he gave a cry and without warning his horse bolted, deserting the avenue for the woods, with the Duc looking as though he might be thrown at any moment.

Oriana pulled up sharply, perplexed. She had always considered that the Frenchman had a good seat, but she had no time to reflect but merely gave chase into the woods as fast as she could. Her horse was one of the late Viscount's finest hunters and she soon caught up with the Duc's hired horse, leaning forward perilously to grasp the reins. The horse stopped, the Duc seemed to lose his seat entirely and tumbled to the ground. For a few seconds, all Oriana could do was attend to the horses, but when she looked, the Duc was lying still on the ground, handsome face turned towards her.

She jumped with unmaidenly agility from her horse, secured them both and ran towards the prone figure. She knelt and put one gloved hand to his brow and was startled to feel his fingers close around her wrist in a vice-like grip.

'Miss Petersham,' he breathed in a thickened voice, 'Ma belle. Mon *ange*.' Suddenly he was on his feet, pulling her to him. She gave a squeal before his lips closed on hers, his arms enveloping her.

Her mind was working furiously; no one could hear her. No doubt he was counting on that. Perhaps, he thought that his kisses would move her. More likely that shame would make her his. She struggled, then went limp. His arms relaxed a little and he took his lips from her to murmur, 'Darling.'

This gave her the opportunity she needed to free her whip hand. She brought it with all her force upon his face. It did not draw blood, but he sprung back, uttering a number of French expletives that Oriana was glad she did not know.

As he sprang forward towards her with a quite different look in his eye, a large horse came bursting through the shrubbery and caused them both to turn. Grandiston, riding towards the main house, had seen the incident from a distance and had followed them into the woods, guided by Oriana's call.

The Frenchman's handsome countenance lost all colour whilst Grandiston's face, seeing the stripe of his cheek, became a hard shell. He did not dismount but rode forward and quite deliberately added a second stripe to his face. This one did bleed, and the Frenchman snarled.

'Go!' ordered the earl, 'And if I ever hear that you have breathed this lady's name you may find that your welcome in England has run out.'

M. Le Duc picked up his hat and mounted his horse, his anger inflamed but his sense of danger keeping him quiet. Grandiston was a friend of the Regent and a return to France was not so safe for him in these times. He rode off without a word.

Grandiston dismounted. Oriana, who had stood without flinching throughout this exchange, began now, unaccountably, to shake. She turned shining eyes towards him, quite forgetting that he was to be guarded against.

'It's silly,' she said looking at him, 'I can't seem to stop.'

He lifted her off her feet and into his arms.

'But …' she protested feebly.

As he felt her trembling with shock his heart gave way and he pulled her tighter. 'Little Pigeon.'

'Ah, don't,' she said looking up at him, 'Don't call me that.' Her eyes began to swim; she felt her weakened defences crumble at the use of his old name for her, and her heart reached out for him.

And then he swung her on to his horse and swung up beside her.

'But Beauty …' she protested.

'… will eat grass until the stable boy fetches him. Now we'll get you home.'

She had no protests left. She thought that she was well enough to ride, but the strange shaking had not yet abated and it was easier by far to slip into the comfort of Grandiston's broad chest and to ignore the question that ran around her head and the feeling that swelled in her chest. She was safe. Grandiston was here. She closed her eyes.

He rode towards the house slowly; aware of the heaviness of her head against him, of her little gloved hand clutching his shirt. The desire to kiss her was outweighed by the desire only to protect her and to kill The Duc de Montaigne. His feelings surprised him; tenderness was an ache in his chest. Still she shook from the attack and though his body was alight with the feel of her, not for a second would he have moved to make her feel uncomfortable at this time.

He rode to the back of the house to avoid uproar. Entering the kitchen, he began to bark orders whilst the servants ran to his commands.

In a few moments, Sullivan was bending over Miss Micklethwaite's ear and she excused herself from the company of Lady Staines and her son, Mr Thorne, Sir Piers and the other ladies.

Grandiston surrendered his charge, saying merely, 'Miss Petersham has had a severe shock.'

He had laid her on her pink silk coverlet and she reached a hand for him as he took his leave, 'Thank you!' she breathed.

He touched it briefly and said, 'Lie still now. It is all over.' With a smile he was gone.

Miss Micklethwaite watched Oriana's eyes follow him and an empty, frightened look appeared as he left. She sat on the bed and before she could speak Oriana sat up and threw herself onto her friend's large bosom, sobbing wildly. She cried for her fear, for her weakness, for the final crumbling of the wall that she had built around herself since her father's death. She cried for love (why hadn't she known it before?) of Grandiston, and not knowing what to do about it.

The older woman wisely said nothing, but held on whilst Oriana's innumerable worries and fears, held in check for so long , spilled out in wracking sobs for a long time.

Eventually, she laid her in her bed and left her to sleep the deep unconscious sleep of the emotionally exhausted.

The morning callers, for the most part disappointed by Miss Petersham's absence, took their leave and it was left to Mr Thorne to entertain the ladies. Miss Micklethwaite entered again unnoticed as he took his position before the fire, grasping his lapels in the way that foretold a speech.

'I must say, Clarissa, that though I did not like this notion of you setting up here, and indeed it is a foolish notion for a young lady to imagine she can run a great estate, your stay here has had some benefits.'

Clarissa, whose face had flushed at this beginning, opened her mouth to reply, when Miss Appleby's gentle voice interceded, 'How silly of me. Clarissa, dear, could you retrieve my blue silk, it has fallen at your feet.' As she returned the thread to the lady who sat so peacefully at her embroidery, she was surprised by a little gesture of a finger to her lips. She remembered her promise to Grandiston and managed to smile slightly at her brother.

'Yes indeed, my dear girl. The company that has seen fit to call has been, well, *elevated* if I may say so. I wrote as much to my dear Cornelia the other day and I had a letter from her this morning.' He looked at his sister as one about to give a great surprise, 'She agrees with me that it is impossible to try to break the Dower House contract for the moment. She means to pay a visit to Ashcroft *herself* in the next two weeks. Well. How is *that* my dear sister?'

'Oh dear!' thought Clarissa, but she said everything that was polite.

'You will be pleased to have such an old friend here, will you not my dear Miss Sowersby?' he added, turning to Juliana.

She had never been an intimate of Mrs Thorne, thinking her a rather pushy woman, but there was little Juliana could say but, 'Delighted.'

'Indeed, indeed,' said Mr Thorne, 'I believe that My Lord Grandiston has expressed a heartfelt wish to meet with my wife. Imagine his happiness at this news.'

'Imagine ...' said Clarissa dryly.

Miss Micklethwaite shot her a warning look. 'Well, John, you should write her a letter expressing Clarissa's joy at the news as quickly as may be. No need to delay her,' she said bracingly.

'Yes, indeed!' said Mr Thorne, leaving the room and beaming.

When he had gone, Clarissa turned to Miss Appleby. 'Thank you so much, dear lady. I almost opened my mouth and I know that I must not. But really, John is *so* infuriating – he told Mr Elfoy that he needn't meet with me anymore - *he* would deal with any business that arose. Can you equal his gall?'

'Well, my dear,' began Miss Appleby, 'I knew you might be betrayed into heated discourse - I was just such an impetuous young lady as you at one time ...' Clarissa raised astonished eyes to the little lady, 'but I found it would never do. I caused my dear papa such shame with my quick tongue...'

'How did you ...' said Clarissa with genuine interest.

'Never mind that,' said Miss Micklethwaite testily, 'Oriana is in bed, Clarissa, I believe you should go to her.'

At the other ladies' exclamations she said very little, but bustled Clarissa from the room.

It was a measure of the change in Oriana that she poured out the entire morning's adventures into her friend's ears within five minutes.

'How could I have been so taken in?' she said, her eyes swimming in tears and her cheeks hot with humiliation. 'I have seen him ride many times; I should have guessed his purpose. But his manner before that was not at all urgent ...' she put her hand over her eyes.

Clarissa pulled them away. 'It is his behaviour that is at fault, not yours. None of us would have guessed his intentions. He thought he was dealing with a weaker willed woman than you, Oriana. He will not be able to show his face in town with those marks on him for a sennight.' She looked at her friend's distress with a mixture of sympathy and an explosive rage that men could act in this way. Petersham, Thorne, du Montaigne, she thought; all the same. Using their power to achieve their own ends with no thought of us.

'It is not like you to blame yourself, Oriana,' said Clarissa. 'Get angry with M. le Duc, not yourself.'

Oriana's lovely face looked raw with emotion. 'Oh, I know,' she said, brokenly, 'it is just that Grandiston must have thought ...'

Clarissa was puzzled. 'Grandiston has shown him to be too much our friend to think meanly of you ... he saw you attack the Duc ... he has been *your* friend for such a long time ...' As she watched her friend wipe her streaming eyes with an inadequate lace handkerchief, she stilled suddenly. 'Oriana, why have you let Grandiston continue to believe that you consented to that ludicrous engagement?'

Oriana's eyes flew to Clarissa's shrewd grey ones, then her eyelids lowered. She sniffed, 'He should *know* ...' she wailed, striving for control between anger and despair.

Clarissa grasped her hands, 'Oh dear, you love him *very* much, don't you?' she said gently.

'*I do not.*'

In her second outburst of feeling that day, Oriana threw herself into Clarissa's arms and cried her heart out.

CHAPTER 15

Dinner for Friends

Over the next few days, spirits returned to normal. Mr Thorne was much improved by the thought of the imminent arrival of his wife, whilst Clarissa and Oriana found a new warmth in their friendship, in which they gladly included Juliana.

Mercifully, Oriana was spared the necessity of meeting the earl, for she did not know if she would give away her feelings. How could she not have known that she had loved him all along? Grandiston still called, but merely to invite Mr Thorne to go riding or to lunch, claiming to miss the society of his friend Booth. The ladies felt the relief, and thus his real intentions.

Clarissa was thus able to meet with Mr Elfoy in the library on a morning that she had instructed Sullivan to deny them to visitors. She met him with her usual friendliness, and an air of conspiracy.

'We may not have a great deal of time, sir,' she said briskly, 'so I beg you look at this.'

It was a set of plans for the closure of the West Wing, sent off, on her instructions, from the architect (mercifully still alive) who had been called in by her uncle when he considered restoring the damaged building.

Elfoy was excited as he bent over the desk with her.

'It looks so simple to close off, just the three doorways to brick up. It is a shame that we cannot begin immediately, but I fear your brother ...'

'But we can,' she interrupted excitedly. She turned towards him impulsively. 'I have thought of a way. If we do not begin soon the work can never be completed before winter sets in. If we keep all the work to the back of the house for now, there is no reason for John to find out.'

'Yes, it could be done,' he said thoughtfully, 'we shall only need a small proportion of the stone and slate after all. But though Mr Thorne does not have the power to order the estate, when he finds out what you wish to do - forgive me, he may simply order you away with him. If only there were any way I could stop him.' This last he said almost to himself, his brows went down and he made his hand into a fist.

Clarissa was amused. 'But we already settled that you cannot,' she said lightly, making fun of their old discomfort. As his eyes flew to hers she felt them sear her and she laughed a little more tremulously, 'Why Mr Elfoy, Tristram, you look quite fierce.'

He lowered his eyes a second, lest all his feeling became naked. 'I beg your pardon, it is just the way he speaks to me of you as though you were little more than the village idiot.

Does he not *know* you? And do not say that it is merely that he speaks of all women thus - for of his wife he can say no ill. I have not met her, but it is easy to see who rules the roost.' He had been pacing the floor whilst Clarissa observed him, her hand to her bosom, but he stopped suddenly. 'I beg your pardon, Miss Thorne. That was completely ...'

'Insightful,' finished Clarissa. She was a little flushed herself but she laughed and placed a calming hand on his arm. 'No need for apologies between such friends as us. Please call me Clarissa, and give me leave to call you by your name. We are too much in union now to stand on ceremony.' He grasped her hands speakingly and looked his gratitude with his eyes.

'It would not be fitting,' he said, with resolve.

'As to that - perhaps not in public. But between ourselves and the ladies I see no harm. Now let me tell you my plan to begin at once, without John's knowledge.'

An hour later, she went gleefully upstairs, pleased with her secret plotting and with a little more that the interview had delivered.

Miss Appleby was coming down, dressed in bonnet and pelisse. 'Dear Appleby - going out again?'

Miss Appleby flushed slightly, 'If you do not need me, my dear. We have no visitors now until dinner this evening. I am going to give Sir Mortimer some of my mother's tisane, which is most efficacious against gout.'

'Give him my regards and tell him I shall call next week, if it is convenient.'

'Oh, yes, dear,' she said a little vaguely. 'Good day.'

She found her two friends in her room, curled onto the bed, looking at back numbers of the periodical *La Belle Assemblée,* thoughtfully sent over by Lady Staines.

Juliana looked up, her face full of mischief. 'My dear, Oriana and I have calculated that it is time for you to wear colour again. We have been looking at these periodicals and we have seen the very dresses for you.'

Clarissa joined them willingly enough, but laughed outright at one of the illustrations. 'I will not be seen in a Turkish bonnet. Lady Staines looked quite odd enough when she greeted us *à la Turque* the other day. I do *not* intend to join her.'

Juliana looked serious, 'Oh, yes, but I truly have seen ladies in Turkish dress who look unexceptionable. It is just her ladyship's sense of colour is a little ... But it is not that dress, but the next. Those simple lines, and in blue, such a good colour for you.' Her gentle voice and artist's eye made Clarissa laugh again.

'That is all very well, but how will I manage? Oriana knows how much work it took to contrive my mourning. A whole other set of clothes is more than I bargained for. Why did I not think? We do not have the leisure to raid what is left of mother's trunk.'

Juliana looked a little conscious. 'Well, as to that ... I have two gowns with me that have never become me. You know that you and I cannot wear the same colours, but I was so impulsive as to cause my dressmaker to make me a French dress in a heavenly blue muslin and another evening gown in white. And I cannot wear white, whatever my mama says is fashionable, I look positively ill.'

She produced the gowns from behind her and Clarissa gasped. The celestial blue was dazzling, a very fine muslin overdress with a silk petticoat, sewn all over with the same coloured flowers. The white heavier satin evening gown was covered by the almost classical drape of white sarcenet embellished in silver.

It was all she could do to refuse, 'I cannot!' she cried.

Oriana began to speak, but Juliana just held the white dress up under her own chin. 'Will you really make me wear this?' she said, eyebrows raised. The others gasped; it seemed all the warm light had faded from Juliana's complexion, to take on the blue tinge of the consumptive.

Oriana giggled, 'Have pity, Clarissa,' she said.

'The blue's worse,' sighed Juliana and soon all three were giggling and Clarissa had agreed to take the gowns. It did not seem so difficult then, to accept some more fashion errors from her beautiful friend Oriana. A jonquil day dress of fine cambric and a muslin gown sprigged with pink peonies, plus some shawls, a blue velvet spencer that went well with several of them, to wear on chill days.

'How fortunate I am not a blonde!' she said.

Oriana moreover recommended that they raid the trunk once more, but this time take its contents, along with some of these illustrations, to the dressmaker in the village whom the useful Lady Staines had already recommended. It seemed, too, that it was not beyond their expenses (now that they had the rent from the Dower House) to buy some lengths of muslin and perhaps a little silk to make a few more gowns 'befitting the first lady of the county' as Juliana reminded her.

This put Oriana in mind that her dresses were over a season old and must need a new touch. So the next few hours were spent in planning what ribbons, trims, reticules, collars and slippers could be dyed, bought or exchanged amongst them to bring the ladies right into fashion.

Dinner that evening was to be cosy affair, with the vicar, Dr Challoner and his amiable wife and daughters, Grandiston, Mr Thorne, the ladies and (at Miss Micklethwaite's invitation) Mr Elfoy and his mother. Mr Thorne had not been best pleased with this last, since his dealings with Mr Elfoy led him to suspect that young man's manner. The agent had replied civilly to Mr Thorne's orders and questions but he had failed to agree to act or to answer. When John had exploded that Elfoy had had a different attitude when first they met, the young man had coolly replied, 'When you acted as Miss Thorne's representative, I did of course give you every aid. Now that Miss Thorne may order me, I am not at liberty to discuss her business.'

The answer may have been blandly business like, the tone mild, but there was a little steel in the eyes that Mr Thorne did not care for from one beneath him. It gave him pause however, and he did not mention it to Clarissa as he meant to. If Elfoy were not also a gentleman, he might have crushed him thoroughly but as it was, he held his tongue.

'Why did you invite Elfoy, ma'am?' he said peevishly to Miss Micklethwaite, as they awaited their guests.

Miss Micklethwaite gave him the condescending look that she had reserved for him since his youth and said, 'I wish to consult with Mrs Elfoy on household matters and as I believe that he and his mother are both friends of Dr and Mrs

Challonerit seemed natural to invite them. From your tone I perceive you have an objection. Out with it, if you please.'

'Well, it is just that that fellow seems always to be here ...' He caught her eye, '...no objection, none at all,' he finished, lamely.

Miss Micklethwaite returned her eye, mercifully, to her needlework.

Clarissa came in wearing the blue gown; her hair caught up in a pretty striped ribbon, in the Grecian style. With Oriana in sea-green gauze and Juliana in pink silk they created a picture as they moved forward.

John cleared his throat to comment, his brows knit at her appearance, but before he could, the guests were announced.

Finally seated beside Grandiston, he glowered at Clarissa across the table. He was really unable to tell how a mousy, plain young bluestocking had transformed into this ever increasingly pretty young lady. Her confident charm with her guests, whilst not appearing too pushing, also alarmed him. Things appeared more and more out of his control, even though he knew of course that they could not be. Clarissa had never minded him, but he thought that with the death of his stepmother he would finally have the upper hand. He knew that he did, but as he sat and watched Clarissa exchange some village gossip with Mrs Challoner, or turn a compliment on the dinner towards Miss Micklethwaite, he did not feel it.

Her gown this evening (no doubt wildly expensive) must have been bought with money that had best have been cared for by him. The young Misses Challoner were compliment-ing her, whilst themselves wearing simple round gowns of muslin: more seemly, in Mr Thorne's opinion. This is what came of young girls having charge of their own finances - it was spent on fripperies. He looked again at the fine muslin and wondered if his own dear wife owned one half so fine.

Grandiston leant over to him and murmured, 'Your sister is at last out of mourning. Charming.'

Mr Thorne's soul warmed a little. Perhaps the earl's unaccountable fancy for Clarissa might deepen.

There was a lull at the table when Mr Challoner said, 'Do you mean to go to London next season, Miss Thorne? Our little social gatherings are not enough for the young, I fear.'

Clarissa was about to speak, when Mr Thorne cleared his throat, 'Ah, I rather think my sister's plans, *any* plans, are uncertain.'

Mr Challoner, sensing the rebuke, coughed discreetly.

Grandiston, however, charged into the opening. 'You must give us your presence in town, indeed, Miss Thorne. The season would not be complete without you.'

'It is kind of you to say so sir, but I fear I have little London acquaintance,' said Clarissa lightly.

Oriana raised her eyebrow slightly in Grandiston's direction, too distracted by curiosity about his tactics to be shy, as she had been earlier. He grinned slightly.

'Nonsense, my dear,' said Grandiston bracingly. 'why, half of London has been parked in your morning room this past week. Miss Petersham's extensive London acquaintance is now yours, quite apart from Miss Sowersby and her family, Mr Booth and I. You cannot want for visitors. Is not that right, Mr Thorne?'

John received his pat on the back with forced good humour. 'Indeed, yes, but no doubt my sister may wish to visit myself this winter.'

'Nonsense, my dear man, you cannot wish to deprive us of Miss Thorne's first appearance in society. The owner of Ashcroft must be seen.'

This did not seem the place to announce that his sister would not long own the estate, so John took refuge in vagueness. 'It would be pleasant dear sister, but then again I believe London lodgings are scurrilously expensive.'

The good, round faced Mrs Challoner, who had never been further than twenty miles hence, shook her head wisely in agreement.

John was about to turn the subject when Mr Elfoy, seated beside his mother and Miss Micklethwaite at the other end of the table, said clearly, 'Well, there is Ashcroft House.'

John, the wineglass to his lips, paused. 'A London House? I did not know of this.'

Clarissa looked at him blandly. 'I had it up for sale, but I suppose I might keep it for one more season,' then seeing that he was most seriously discomposed, she began to back-track. 'However, I've always thought that without a presentation at court and so on, there is no point in a London season. I have no London family to present me, so it looks like I shall have to forfeit the whole idea.'

Mr Thorne's wineglass continued to his mouth.

'Not necessarily,' said Mr Elfoy clearly. His third glass of wine was making him a little reckless, he felt, but he enjoyed Thorne's face losing that self-satisfied look. He watched, with satisfaction, as it changed colour now. Then he turned to the lady whom Mr Thorne had hardly acknowledged this evening, 'Mama?'

The sweet lady beside him raised her serene head and said, 'Of course.' As the company, bar Dr and Mrs Challoner, looked astonished, she smiled deprecatingly. 'It is just that my sister, Lady Carmichael, is a Lady-in-Waiting to dear Queen Charlotte.' Grandiston's brows raised and Thorne's jaw dropped, 'I am very sure she could procure an invitation to the presentation for dear Miss Thorne. And present her, of course.' She smiled warmly across the table at Clarissa, who looked dumbfounded.

'You are too kind, my dear Mrs Elfoy. I must admit that I am astonished that I have such a very varied acquaintance.'

Grandiston's brows knit, 'Ah, you are a Darlington then, a fine Staffordshire family. I knew your brother well and his son a little. Do you travel to town much?'

Mrs Elfoy looked a little conscious. 'When my health permits: short visits only to the family. When I married Tristram's father, I chose the quiet country life and I have never regretted it.'

John Thorne looked dumbfounded, 'But a court presentation ...' he spluttered, '... surely it is not possible...'

Mrs Elfoy looked at him and for a second Clarissa could see a hint of some distaste cross her face but her tone was gentle as she said, 'Nothing could be simpler, I assure you.'

Miss Appleby, who had been a little quiet, this evening, became enlivened at this news.

'Oh, dear Mrs Elfoy - how wonderful! A presentation at court for my dear Miss Thorne - just as her mamma should have wished. Well ... that is to say ...' she coloured a little, and came to a halt.

'What Miss Appleby means, Mrs Elfoy, was that my mother might have wished it if she had given a thought to anything but books,' said Clarissa with humour.

'Clarissa!' said her brother sharply, but the conversation had overtaken him.

'Scholarship is a very laudable activity,' said Mr Challoner, 'and there have been throughout history many examples of women scholars ...'

'Yes,' Clarissa, 'Mamma referred to them often.' She wrinkled her nose thoughtfully, 'But I do think that though a pattern of womanhood in many ways, it would have been more *practical* if Mama had remembered to arrange things like my coming out, or a court presentation.'

Anyone choosing to look at Mr Elfoy at this precise moment (as it happened Juliana was) could not help but see the look of glowing admiration he cast at the unaware Clarissa. Tonight, in blue with blue beads dripping from her naked shoulders, she was even more beautiful than before. Miss Sowersby was pretty, Miss Petersham a cool beauty, but neither had the animation and vivacity that Clarissa exuded. And today she had called him a friend. Then he grinned. She was so impulsive and honest in a way young ladies had been taught not to be. Even his mother smiled behind her napkin at her latest speech, whilst her brother was once again enraged.

Mr Thorne cleared his outraged throat to reprimand such outspokenness, when Juliana surprised herself for the second time by drawing his fire.

'It was at her coming out in Harrogate that you first met dear Mrs Thorne, was it not?' she said a little more loudly than was her want.

Mr Elfoy gave her a look of real admiration and Clarissa gave her one of real gratitude.

Thorne was diverted and smiled on her in a fawning way and proceeded to tell her the very dull tale (excepting to him, and possibly Miss Appleby, the queen of all romantics) of the first meeting between himself and his dear Cornelia. This naturally led on to her imminent arrival and thus it was fully the sweet course before he stopped talking.

The ladies withdrew to the front drawing room in due course, Clarissa shyly admitting to Mrs Elfoy that she had no real plans to go to London.

'I fear it was the uncustomary mischievousness of my son in bating your brother, I can only apologize,' she whispered back, as they entered the green room. 'Should you change your mind, only a line to me and I shall write to my sister.' She pulled Clarissa a little aside to say with a hesitant smile, 'I fear my son has a deal more pride in his lineage than means.'

Clarissa laid a hand on her arm and replied quietly, but in the most natural way possible, 'I must admit that that is my position, too. Proud of all this - but not so much of the debts.' They exchanged confiding grins and walked forward to the fire, arm in arm.

'Well,' thought Miss Micklethwaite observing this, 'If only a courtship was possible, this would be going very well.'

Juliana and Oriana exchanged speaking glances.

The young Misses Challoners' whispered conversations were in admiration of the Earl of Grandiston, but their secret glances had been for Mr Elfoy. Clarissa had seen him joust good-naturedly with Charlotte - just seventeen - and talk in a different tone with her sister Annabel whose eyes sought him throughout dinner.

It was evident to the occupants of Ashcroft that Mr Elfoy was the most sought after young man in the neighbourhood. Juliana thought it inevitable, since not even in the metropolis had she seen a finer specimen. He could be both sensible and light-hearted, his manners were excellent and yet he contained that hint of strength well-leashed that females could not fail to find irresistible, though Juliana found it a little alarming. It now transpired that his birth was even better than had been supposed and had it not been for the lack of fortune his passion for Clarissa (which had been discussed by all the other Ashcroft ladies) might be the best thing for all. As it was, if Mr Thorne were to get a hint, he'd pack his sister off, earl or no earl.

CHAPTER 16

Cornelia Arrives

Clarissa saw Mr Elfoy only briefly in the next few days and never alone. Her brother had not liked something in the tone of Elfoy's dealings with Clarissa and had gone so far as to give her a warning on the matter. This had been met with such blank incomprehension by his sister that Thorne thought he had better leave such delicate matters to his darling wife. His close attention to Clarissa's movements had a benefit - he was not abroad enough to wonder at the increased activity at the back of the house. She whispered as much to Elfoy over the teacup she was pouring, and he managed to grin, 'Don't worry, I've instructed the men to play gormless yokels if asked what they are up to.'

Clarissa gave a gurgle of laughter, which she translated into a cough, for the benefit of her brother. Her fingers touched Elfoy's as she passed him his cup and she had the silliest wish to leave them there. She blushed a little and lowered her eyes from his suddenly hot gaze.

It is quite, quite impossible, he reminded himself and he moved away with a face of stone. Miss Micklethwaite, observing, felt the need to jab at her stitching with new ferocity.

John had made it plain to Clarissa that he thought the presence of Mr Elfoy could be disposed of at tea, but it seemed that he delivered estate messages in the afternoon. He either contrived to arrive with the earl or was begged by one of the other ladies to join them. John was still frowning at him when Sullivan entered and announced his wife.

'Cornelia!' he exclaimed delightedly.

Cornelia was taking off her gloves and wearing an expression designed to be pleasing. She took in the room's occupants at a glance and moved to give her husband her small hand. She was dressed in a stylish green carriage dress that had cost her devoted husband a substantial sum. However, one look at the London elegance of Misses Sowersby and Petersham and at Clarissa's astonishing new look (Oriana's discarded figured muslin with Brussels lace trim plus a new twist to her Grecian hairstyle achieved by Becky's astonishing budding talent) made her feel slightly sick. She was not much better dressed than those ridiculous companions, she thought, casting a look at Micklethwaite's simple but well-cut cambric and Miss Appleby's sprigged muslin (the fabric discovered in a cache upstairs). Her smile did not waver for a second though, as she was greeted by the ladies. 'Dearest sister,' she said tenderly to Clarissa and then, turning to her neighbour, 'Miss Sowersby, may I call you Juliana?' This increase in intimacy, not to be attempted in the presence of Juliana's parents, was not easily denied.

The earl, sipping tea by the fire watched her carefully. An encroaching mushroom, he thought, such as he knew how to keep at a distance. She showed her lack of breeding in her slighting of Mr Elfoy, who fell back with a contemptuous curl to his lip. It would be a new experience for Grandiston to allow her to encroach. Not too easily, though, he thought as he went forward to be introduced. He gave her a cool smile and a look that seemed to find her pretty plump person somewhat lacking. He bowed graciously enough however and murmured, 'Charmed.'

Juliana marvelled yet again at the easy adoption of his London manners and thought that Mr Booth would have enjoyed how his friend's behaviour increased Mrs Thorne's awe of his titled personage. The earl and Mr Elfoy left swiftly, being delayed by invitations from Mr and Mrs Thorne to come again. 'How kind of you, ma'am,' said Elfoy affecting to misunderstand, 'I will.' He was rewarded by seeing Clarissa's face, strained since Cornelia's entrance, lighten to a grin. Oriana's stately countenance dropped to gurgle into her handkerchief.

'It is so nice of you, my Lord, to be so kind to my dear, sweet sister,' intoned Cornelia, smiling fondly at Clarissa in a way that made that sister wish to box her ears. Oriana squeezed her arm warningly.

'Nonsense, it is I who am in Miss Thorne's debt,' retorted the earl smiling at Clarissa in such a flirtatious way as to make her drop her eyes in a maidenly fashion to disguise a giggle 'She has entertained my friend Booth and I royally.'

Cornelia's breast swelled in hope. This looked most promising. The earl definitely was interested, unbelievably, in John's pert little sister. She could almost see certain individuals in Sowersby who had treated her curtly unbend when they heard that she was related to the Earl of Grandiston. The money coming to her household from the sale of this estate might be restricted to the length of Clarissa's engagement, but wouldn't the earl make a much more handsome settlement upon her family? And the social opportunities of being the sister-in–law of a countess were enough to make her head swim.

Much of this she conveyed to her husband in the comfortable coze they had as they dressed for dinner. They must foster the earl's interest in their dear sister, she felt, for Clarissa's own good.

'Yes, my dear, but what about the house sale?' said her husband worriedly.

'You will secure that at once my love, even if the actual purchase is delayed by a month or so. That should be easily done, for you said that Lord Staines was anxious to complete.'

'But ... my dear, I must tell you that Clarissa is become a little turned by all this admiration ... she may not sign the deed.' He looked shamefaced and worried and Cornelia patted his hand reassuringly.

'You may leave her to me, my dear,' she said confidently, with a little icy spark in her eye, 'I know just how to deal with Clarissa.'

Mr Thorne rested in the balm of the stronger character, just glad that his dear wife had arrived.

Arrive she had. The next day, it seemed to the ladies that Cornelia was everywhere. At breakfast she announced her intention of touring the house. Clarissa bit back her annoyance and professed herself pleased to accompany her.

'Oh no my dear, I shouldn't dream of disturbing you. I shall just get the housekeeper to accompany me.'

Clarissa opened her mouth to object, but found her toe under Miss Appleby's such that she almost yelped. So the aging housekeeper, Mrs Smith, rescued from retirement on the estate by Sullivan, was suffered to walk up and down stairs as Cornelia poked and prodded her way around a grander house than she had ever known. Her manner to her inferiors was haughty in the extreme (giving away her lack of breeding in Mrs Smith's opinion) and she asked probing questions about the house and the contents and the inhabitants in a manner that elicited monosyllabic answers from the old retainer.

Very soon she prised the keys from the housekeeper's hands, a thing Mrs Smith reported she would not have permitted if the stair walking had not given her palpitations. 'I'm sure I travel the reaches of this house every week, Mr Sullivan, in performance of my dooties, but I'm too old to be doing that in an hour.'

And so it was that Cornelia pried her way into every room in the wing. She unlocked linen cupboards and priced the linens and laces to within a penny, she noted the silver and the paintings and furniture and hangings. No legal inventory could have been as complete. Finally, without any compunction, she inspected each of the ladies' rooms.

In Miss Micklethwaite's she found little to interest her: just simple round gowns for the most part and a couple of sensible woollen shawls. At a small desk that that lady had caused to be brought in, she found some letters. She read these with no reserve and made the disturbing discovery that the Micklethwaite woman was sister to a solicitor. Very possibly a low sort of man, but perhaps the letter could be construed dangerously. He made mention of a visit '... to discuss this complicated business in person', could this be something to do with her sister-in–law? Possibly not; but as well to be on guard.

In Miss Appleby's chamber she found as many as six elegant dresses and twelve lace handkerchiefs. A schoolteacher, she thought bitterly. How could she ever deserve this finery?

She was interrupted in her perusal of the handkerchief drawer by an exclamation at the door. Miss Appleby stood, quite pink on the doorstep, staring with shocked eyes at Mrs Thorne.

'Ah, Miss Appleby - is this *your* room?' said Cornelia sweetly.

'Why, yes. Can I help you Mrs Thorne?

Her shocked tone made Cornelia colour just a little, but she replied in an even sweeter voice, 'I am surprised. I should have thought it the late duchess' boudoir, so many treasures does it hold.' She held up a lace handkerchief, cobweb fine and raised an enquiring eyebrow.

'Those were bequeathed to me by my dear Mrs Thorne ...' Appleby stammered apologetically. 'I believe they belonged to her mother, the previous duchess ...' She looked quite distracted and her voice tailed away.

'Really?' said Cornelia, 'My dear step-mamma-in-law left me nothing quite so fine ...'

Miss Appleby looked miserable. 'Perhaps you would like to take ... as a memento ...'

'Not at all, my dear lady,' she said and dropped the handkerchief on the bureau. 'And did my mother-in-law make you a gift of all your handsome dresses?' she asked, smiling her sticky-sweet smile.

'Well, no. Dear Miss Thorne made over some of her mother's gowns ... I hope you do not think that I have imposed on her generosity ...' Miss Appleby sank her head into her hands.

Cornelia bustled forward and took Miss Appleby's hands in hers. 'My dear lady, of course not! I have no doubt you wish to be great help to my sister - but I am here now. If you have behaved *thoughtlessly* in accepting gifts that Clarissa simply cannot afford, I absolve you of any blame in the matter. I know how forceful the young can be. However, it really *won't do*, will it? And staying in this house whilst being of little use to Clarissa ... well, I shall leave you to think about it. There now ....' And with a final pat of the miserable Appleby's hands, she left to enter Clarissa's room.

She was full of rage as she explored the cupboards and presses of the most magnificent bedchamber she had ever seen. The morning fire that Becky thought only due to Clarissa's dignity was glowing still in the grate and the silver brushes, combs and perfume bottles glittered on the elegant French dressing table. The dresses were like a slap in the face to her. Finer muslins and silks met her eyes than she herself possessed. That at least four of them were gifts from Oriana and Juliana she neither knew nor cared. They represented the way in which Clarissa had been catapulted above her in status and wealth, the way in which she had exerted her independence over her brother, who would certainly not have let her fritter her money away on such finery.

With tumultuous jealousy she moved onto the next bedroom, which turned out to be Oriana's. The sheer luxury and quantity of Oriana's possessions caused the acid in her stomach to rise. How could this be? On the only previous occasion that she had met Oriana, she had been in that dreadful little school, working, and now she was lording it in fine clothes that outdid Juliana's, the wealthiest young lady of Cornelia's acquaintance. As she stooped over to examine more closely a silk shawl, very likely worth thirty pounds and more she heard a rustle at the door. She stood up before turning towards the door slowly, appearing to be quite mistress of the situation. 'I am afraid I got rather lost in the corridors my dear, such a large house. I thought this was my sweet sister Clarissa's room, but I fear I am wrong.' She gave a false laugh, 'So sorry.'

Oriana inclined her head, her anger at the intrusion hidden behind a mask-like stare that began to put Cornelia a little out of countenance. She looked down and found her fingers still held the shawl, 'What a pretty treasure, I'm sure I do not know what such a pretty thing might cost.'

Oriana let her eyes rest on Cornelia's unexciting shawl and curled her lip, 'How should you, to be sure?' Cornelia blushed at the slight.

'At any rate, it must be beyond a school-teacher's yearly salary,' she said challengingly.

Oriana raised her eyelids a little, 'Do you wish to borrow it?' she asked with chilling civility, 'I believe I have another two or three that might better suit your gown.'

Cornelia was enraged. 'Do you mean to tell me that my sister has made you a present of *four* such shawls? She cannot have squandered such an amount ...'

'Mrs Thorne, I do not mean to tell you anything at all as I can see no earthly reason why it is any of your business. You'd better hurry to get dressed, ma'am. Luncheon will be served shortly.' And she held the door open regally for the defeated one to leave.

Cornelia's rage sought relief and she took it when she saw the door of Miss Appleby's room ajar, she looked in and saw the poor lady weeping into one of the handkerchiefs that had excited her jealousy.

'My dear lady, please do not distress yourself so,' she cooed, 'Much better to write to your brother – Farnham, is it not - to apprise him of your arrival.'

Miss Appleby wiped her eyes distractedly, 'Yes, oh yes. That is just what I should do. Th-thank you, Mrs Thorne.'

Cornelia swept downstairs, her self-satisfaction reborn.

Miss Appleby sat down to write a letter to her relatives and found herself instead dashing off a note to Sir Montague. She felt it would be so impolite of her to leave the county without informing him of her regret at not seeing him again. Once she had finished this missive she was, for some strange reason, wholly overset and she found herself unable to write the dreaded letter to Farnham. Resolving to do it later, she went downstairs and laid her note on the hall table for Sullivan to deal with, being drawn to raise it to her lips fleetingly before she put it down.

'That is quite enough of that,' she thought briskly, blinking a little before turning to look at Waity, who was addressing her.

'My dear,' she was saying conspiratorially, 'We must go to the hothouses directly. Some of the ex-soldiers that Mr Elfoy has rounded up are to be put to work there and we must get them organized. Are you quite alright? You look a little peaked.'

'Quite all right, my dear. Oh, the poor wretches. They cannot find work elsewhere because of their injuries, Mr Elfoy says, and are only too happy to work on the estate for a cottage and their keep. I shall come at once.'

'Quietly now,' said Mrs Micklethwaite, 'we do not want that dreadful woman to know what we are at. She has been everywhere today.'

'Yes, she has,' said Miss Appleby, but so softly that her friend did not hear her.

CHAPTER 17

The Ball

The behaviour of Miss Appleby was a little strained for the rest of her busy day; Clarissa found her dashing away tears in the stillroom whilst Juliana and Oriana were worried at her stumbling fingers when they joined her to help mend the linen mountain in the little schoolroom. It had been Sullivan's excellent suggestion to have a fire lit there, so as the ladies could 'have a little privacy, if they liked'. They liked very well.

Oriana set her tongue to lashing the under-bred behaviour of Clarissa's sister-in-law, and Juliana, though less strident, could not approve of how Mrs Thorne was taking over.

'She is not much liked in Sowersby, I'm afraid,' she acknowledged, 'She treats her inferiors so shabbily. The dear Miss Monkton's invited her to tea last year - you know, bread and butter sandwiches and ancient linen from their grandmother - and she behaved appallingly, I heard. The

Misses Monktons were so upset that they cancelled their 'At-Homes' for a fortnight and it was only when Mamma begged an invitation of them that they started up again.'

'Dreadful!' said Oriana, 'she wants to make herself feel better by making everyone else, no matter how worthy, feel awful.'

'Do you really think so, my dear?' said Miss Appleby hopefully, 'But perhaps she is only acting for the best, for Clarissa's sake. She is, after all, family,' she added forlornly, and stabbed her finger again with her needle.

Sir Montague's man, meanwhile, had reached Mr Elfoy and summoned him to his house. The news that he imparted, with great upset and bluster, Elfoy took at once to the Dower House. He entered through the French doors, very much at his ease now.

'That blasted woman -' he exclaimed to Grandiston, who was standing by the fire.

'Oh, Elfoy,' said the earl suavely, 'did my housekeeper set her dog on you again? You've joined a happy company,' he gestured to Mr and Mrs Thorne and Clarissa, seated in the high backed chairs.

Mr Elfoy's face was wooden, but a glance at Clarissa's almost overcame him. It was alive with glee. Grandiston cocked him an eyebrow, but he managed a tolerable bow and said what was proper.

'I think,' said Cornelia regally, 'that it is time we left, my love.' She turned and smiled simperingly at Grandiston, 'You must tell Lord Staines we shall be delighted to attend the ball, although whether the other ladies shall be able to attend, I do not know.'

'Oh, I think they will,' said Grandiston suavely, 'I depend upon all of you attending or I shall find that Mr Booth and I have another engagement that evening.'

Cornelia paused. 'Oooh, you,' she said eventually, 'of course, if that is the way of it, I shall do my very best to persuade them. But it is not at all what they are used to as schoolteachers, you know, and they will be overwhelmed, I daresay,' she added with a sidelong look to see how he took this argument.

Grandiston smiled and kissed her hand, 'But something tells me what Mrs Thorne wants, she gets. I leave it to you to persuade them.'

She laughed and turned her pretty head, not sure that she had seen and heard the steel in the earl's eye and voice, but certainly not prepared to take the chance. She led the way out of the door, but in response to the pregnant look in Mr Elfoy's eye, Clarissa ran back in, on the pretext of forgetting a glove.

'Can you get the ladies here without being spotted?' he said urgently, automatically clutching her hands. Grandiston looked on benignly. They gave themselves away so easily, these two.

'All of them?' whispered Clarissa, laughing.

'As many as possible - and soon.'

Cornelia was saying to John, 'A Ball. Oh, John I never thought for so much diversion when I came to this house. And do you not think Grandiston is paying a great deal of distinguishing attention to Clarissa - she could be a countess within the year.'

John looked pleased, 'Yes, but dear one, should we not get back home to the children soon? We should settle this estate sale as soon as possible.'

'Yes, of course arrange it with Staines, but set the date a month or two forward, we would not like to let a chance like this slip by. When Clarissa marries Grandiston there is no saying what good it may do us.' A new hope dawned, 'Would there not be settlements?'

John blushed. 'Surely not. I am not her father after all.'

'Yes, but you are the nearest relative. Oh John, we would be made.'

Clarissa joined them and conversation reverted to the ball and whilst she answered desultorily, she was wondering how to round up and smuggle four women out to the Dower House. Various remedies, including Miss Micklethwaite scaling a rope ladder, occurred only to be gigglingly dismissed.

The landaulet carriage it would have to be, round at the back of the house, taking the small road through the trees, where the tradesmen came. She supposed it must connect to the Dower House somewhere.

So it was that the ladies met in the Dower House a bare half hour later.

Mr Elfoy drew Miss Appleby away and spoke quietly to her.

'Sir Montague has informed me of your decision to leave.'

Miss Appleby grasped his wrist and shushed him, 'I pray you be quiet sir,' she begged, 'I would not have Clarissa know for the world. You see Mrs Thorne has made me see that it is the right thing to do but my dear child could never be brought to acknowledge it.' Her little eyes pleaded desperately to him and he felt an overwhelming urge to damn both the Thornes to perdition. This queer old thing might almost be his mother and he was damned if he would allow that poisonous woman to hurt her like this.

'I will say nothing, upon my honour,' he said, knowing he could rely on Sir Montague if Clarissa had to know, 'But I must ask you for a favour, my dear lady. You must not leave until after the ball. Miss Thorne needs you so. Have you written to the Farnhams yet? Can you put them off?'

Miss Appleby's desire to put the entire thing off altogether vied for place with her sense of duty. 'I really must leave, Mr Elfoy. Mrs Thorne was quite correct.' Her speech became shaken, 'It is so kind of you to...'

'Indeed, ma'am, I am not being kind,' he said, grasping her wringing hands in his warm ones, 'I do not know if Miss Thorne can manage to live with her brother's wife without you to support her spirits. Indeed, she has told me as much.' His warm voice soothed her and she looked up at him.

'Do you think so indeed?' she said hopefully, 'Mrs Thorne is a little forceful, although I am sure that Clarissa has quite enough spirit to deal with her. But perhaps she might need me to alter the ball gown ... and the linen is still in such a state ... Perhaps I shall delay writing to my relatives for a little while.' She smiled at him hazily, and he led her into the drawing room, where everyone sat under the spell of Grandiston holding court.

The results of this conference were not seen until a week later, the night of the ball.

The number of candles employed by Lady Staines to light the ballroom would not have disgraced the most ambitious

London hostess. Her son might have quibbled about the ruinous cost for a mere country ball, but news that his mother had received from the capital about the exact incredible total of Miss Petersham's fortune had relaxed his frown. That the beauty who had smitten him enough to ignore her portion came also with such birth and fortune took his breath away.

He had been obliged to invite some of his rivals for his beloved's hand, but since the strange disappearance of the French Duc, he felt himself to be preeminent on the list. He had enough self-satisfaction to be unable to doubt his own victory. His mother, dressed tonight in hot pink and purple, was not so confident, but she resolved to do her best to secure this catch for her boy.

Oriana looked magnificent this evening. Her ball gown was of simple white silk embroidered subtly with silver butterflies that caught the light as she moved. At her neck was a single pearl drop while her hair was piled in a classical style and held by white satin ribbons. Every gentleman in the room stared unashamedly whilst even the most charitable ladies felt a twinge of envy.

Clarissa, standing in her shadow and taking in the reaction with an amused smile, found one pair of eyes meet hers. Mr Elfoy, resplendent in plain evening dress and white satin waistcoat appeared to have glanced at the apparition very quickly, in favour of looking at Oriana's companion. She blushed. She was looking rather dashing herself, she thought, (though best not to stand next to Oriana if she wished anyone to note it). Her hair was coiled and allowed to escape in shining curls onto her neck and her dress of cerulean blue crepe cut daringly at her bosom became her well and opened at the front over a white satin under-dress. Blue ribbon of the same shade adorned her curls and she looked, to Mr Elfoy's eye, quite perfect. Evidently agreeing, Sir Piers came forward to lead her into the dance-set just forming. Since he had not even requested Miss Petersham as yet, Elfoy knew this to be fatally significant. So he had nothing better to do then than accidentally to break the heart of one of the vicar's daughters whilst raising the hopes of the second by leading her to the set, manfully avoiding following Clarissa with his gaze but quite missing the melting looks his companion was giving him.

Miss Micklethwaite, in the plainest of black silks, wondered if Grandiston had *that* situation in his grand plan. She looked over at him, whilst he stood languidly listening to one of the London swains and gazing at the dance. Unexpectedly, he met her eye after his gaze had been directed at Elfoy. What she saw there allowed her to release a little sigh. There was a man, she thought. One she could depend on, though she had never before done so. She gazed at Oriana, being led by Lord Staines to the dance floor with her face showing as much animation as a corpse. I hope Grandiston has an eye to his own affairs, she thought.

There was a party of late arrivals at the ball, two uninvited, but Grandiston had dropped a word in Lady Staines' ear, so she moved forward royally, 'Mr Booth and Mr and Mrs Sowersby, I believe. You are most welcome, how lovely that you could come after your long journey.'

Mr Sowersby, in a plain but excellently cut evening dress, bent over her hand suavely, 'Forgive the imposition Lady

Staines, but my wife is anxious to see her daughter again after the weeks of her visit.'

Lady Staines looked from young Booth, whose eyes were searching the room, to Mrs Sowersby, 'Ah, a romance.'

Mrs Sowersby smiled. 'You have guessed it. We have visited Mr Booth's family on our way here, but it is not to be announced yet. Ah, there is my dear girl, but who is she dancing with?'

'Oh, Sir Piers Loxley,' uttered her ladyship with a warm feeling of having the most fashionable country ball in recorded history.

Booth had discovered Juliana also, and led her parents forward to the dance hall. When she saw them, she gave a little squeal, and apologised to her partner. He was amused and good naturedly led her from the floor.

'Is all well, Mamma?' said Juliana worriedly.

'All is well, my dear. There is only the argument about the timing - Mr Booth wishes to wed you before Christmas, whilst I am determined not to lose you for a year yet.'

They withdrew to an anteroom, Juliana hardly able to look at her beloved, for fear she would die of her happiness. But soon he was holding her hand and she looked up at him with such shining eyes that Mr Sowersby was made to remark, 'I think, my dear, that it had best be before Christmas.'

Juliana smiled, but then looked conscious, 'Oh, I have a great deal to do here tonight, my dear Mr Booth - and so do you.'

Her mother frowned, but Juliana added, 'It is a plot of Lord Grandiston's, Mamma, I am pledged to secrecy.' She looked mischievously at her mother.

Mrs Sowersby could wish that she had been on such easy terms with the earl in London, but that could not be helped. That august personage could still be of immense social value to the young couple and she would not put herself in the way of any scheme of his.

'What's this?' said the more upright Mr Sowersby.

'Oh Father, 'tis only a scheme to best Mrs Thorne ...' Juliana whispered in his ear.

'Oh,' said her upright parent, remembering several scores good manners had stopped him settling with that lady, 'If that's all ...' And he led them back into the ballroom, whistling.

Mrs Thorne spotted the Sowersbys at once. She felt instantly deflated from the lady-of-the-great-house manner that she had adopted towards the guests all evening. In Sowersby she was minor gentry. She stiffened her sinews: her dear sister-in-law's inheritance had changed her position. Ashcroft was three times the size of Sowersby Manor, and she was family there. Indeed, she had wondered with John the other night whether they could not all move to Ashcroft, for she would like excessively to lord it over the village and manor houses permanently. John, however, had explained that the estate could never recover, that she would have to live without many things and that Clarissa's imprudence so far had probably made things a great deal worse, so she had to abandon the thought. For this evening, though, she would shine. Therefore she went forward to the Sowersbys with an air of the *grande dame,* 'Mr and Mrs Sowersby, how delightful to see you both - Juliana did not tell me you were expected.'

Mrs Sowersby narrowed her eyes at the familiarity and her manner and barely touched her outstretched hand. 'Why should she indeed?'

Clarissa, coming from the dance floor heard this and choked. 'My dear Mr and Mrs Sowersby - how delightful to see you.'

Mr Sowersby had been fond of Clarissa since she had befriended his shy daughter and now he grasped her hands warmly. 'Well my beauty, let's look at you.' He smiled, 'You look fine as fivepence. I declare if it wasn't for those naughty eyes, I should not have known you.'

Clarissa twinkled up at him, 'Do you like my fine new dress?' Cornelia gasped at the effrontery, but Mr Sowersby laughed.

'Very fetching! The latest thing,' he said approvingly

'I am *so* glad, sir, for you paid for it,' she said mischievously.

Mrs Sowersby laughed, 'Oh – it is the blue that did not become Juliana. I declare I did not recognise it, dear Clarissa, so delightful does it look upon you.'

'Minx!' said Sowersby to Clarissa, pinching her chin.

She turned to Charles, 'Well, Mr Booth, I trust you prospered on your journey?' But she was teasing. His smile and familiarity with Juliana's family spoke it all. He winked.

Mrs Thorne drew attention to herself once more. 'You must stay with us, of course, while you are in the district.'

Mr Sowersby gave her a stately bow, 'Miss Thorne has already issued an invitation by way of Mr Booth, but our bags are at the Dower House.'

'Oh,' said Cornelia, shooting a glance of dislike at Clarissa, 'You are well acquainted with Mr Booth, then.'

'He is my daughter's husband-to-be,' said Sowersby indifferently. With a bow, he drew his party away from Mrs Thorne and towards the supper room.

'I could eat a horse,' the Honourable Charles was saying, with Juliana's hand tucked safely into his arm.

They were intercepted by Sir Rodney Pierce, whose pursuit of Oriana had allowed him to meet the gentle Miss Sowersby, also an heiress. 'My dance, I think, Miss Sowersby,' he demanded.

'Sheer off, Fudge,' said Booth, using his schoolboy name, 'Taking my fiancé to supper,' he finished proudly. Sir Rodney shook his hand as did a few persons in the vicinity who had overheard. Juliana blushed rosily and smiled her thanks, being rescued by Clarissa.

'We have settled on the conservatory at eleven, don't fail me,' Clarissa whispered.

Booth raised an eyebrow at his lady love, who squeezed his arm and said, 'I'll tell you later,' in a stage whisper. What was there, wondered Juliana, that made her feel so brave and safe when Charles was beside her? He laughed down at her, entranced by her mischievousness.

By five to eleven, their work had been set in play. The earl had danced twice with Clarissa and had escorted her to supper – conferring an almost unknown distinction. He laughed and teased her and, in one unbelievable moment, Clarissa exclaimed, 'Oh, my shawl, I believe it is in the ballroom!' and turned her wide eyes on her escort. To which the earl had replied, 'Allow me, Miss Thorne,' and marched off to find it.

Both Miss Micklethwaite and Miss Appleby had been quizzed by the ladies present, but had kept their council, mysteriously silent. Had the Earl of Grandiston, pursued by every beauty on the marriage mart for years, finally succumbed to the heiress of Ashcroft? The ballroom was fairly humming. Cornelia overheard several conversations on the subject and John had been asked outright by Sir Piers.

'Oh, my goodness,' said Cornelia to her perplexed husband. 'Everyone is talking about it. They believe he has proposed already.'

'He would naturally have informed me -' said John.

'Well, yes, my love. But his attentions are most marked.'

'If only Clarissa will not refuse him.'

'Refuse him? Grandiston? Even Clarissa could not be so wilful, so ungrateful ...' Cornelia spat out.

'I see nothing more in her manner than her usual kind of banter. The stupid education her mother gave her has left her with no appreciation of rank,' said John worriedly. 'She sent him for her shawl, for goodness sake. Grandiston!'

'I know, but he *went*. Her manners seem to delight him. Oh John - to be visitors at Grandiston Park!'

On this heady thought Mr Booth, who seldom danced, led his wife onto the floor.

CHAPTER 18

The plot

At five to eleven, Charles meandered over to Thorne, who was standing beside a flower arrangement watching his wife dance gaily with a handsome military man.

'Could we withdraw, Thorne?' he said, *sotto* voice.

Mr Thorne looked his amazement.

'You know the Sowersbys well, don't you? Well, I have some advice to ask you.'

John bowed his head in his stiff way and followed Booth's leisurely path towards the conservatory. As they approached the threshold, Charles chatted easily.

'I suppose you know by now that I am affianced to Miss Sowersby? Well, I was hoping you could tip me the wink about old Sowersby? I mean is he ...?'

A sob made Thorne look up, and Clarissa pushed past him from the depths of the conservatory, clutching a handkerchief to her face. As he turned in astonishment, he saw

Juliana sweep his sister into her arms and lead her away to a side room before the ballroom herd could see her distress.

Thorne looked again as another figure emerged from the conservatory: Grandiston. His desire to reprimand a man for taking his sister apart in this way was retarded by the earl's magnificence and it was just as well, for Miss Micklethwaite, ever the chaperone, emerged from behind a large potted palm and curtsied lightly to the earl who nodded.

As that lady joined Miss Appleby who seemed to be hovering nearby – really, was everyone around the conservatory? – he heard her whisper, 'He'll sheer off, for sure.'

Miss Appleby moaned and clucked and the two ladies moved off.

Grandiston was addressing him. 'Your sister has just told me that she must leave the district shortly. That is ... a pity.' His face was unusually grave. 'That is to say, Booth and I are so settled at the Dower House.'

He nodded his head to Thorne and drew Charles away to the ballroom saying, with his old suavity, 'I hear congratulations are in order, dear boy. Let us to the champagne.'

Mr Thorne's thoughts of untold social advancement lay shattered on the floor. He hastened to his wife's side, pouring out the tale in a whisper, interrupted by social smiles to the other guests.

Cornelia found Juliana soothing her sister-in-law in a small ante-chamber.

She swept in, rage repressed, and said to Clarissa. 'Your brother has told me all. Am I to believe, Clarissa, that you have rejected Lord Grandiston?'

Clarissa howled and threw herself onto Juliana's shoulder. Juliana winced, and then turned to Cornelia, her eyes widened in a repressive message. 'You are mistaken, Mrs Thorne, no offer to your sister has yet been received from his lordship.'

Clarissa's sobs increased.

'Tell me at once what has occurred?'

'Nothing has occurred,' replied Juliana even more repressively, 'To be sure we all hoped, when his lordship realised ... but it is best we do not talk of such things just now.'

'Yes. Well. Take care of her and stop her crying.' She swept out once more.

'Clarissa you have quite bruised me,' Juliana said.

'I had to hide my face. I couldn't squeeze out another fake tear.' She grinned. 'Do you think this might actually work?'

'If Mrs Thorne is not trembling at the thought of losing the biggest fish she has ever had on a hook, I've been mistaken in her.'

'So fortunate that Grandiston has such a devious mind.'

Both ladies giggled and set themselves to find some cards to while away a quarter hour before which they could not re-enter the ballroom.

Oriana, meanwhile, was warming up to her role. With great ease, Grandiston had removed her from the coterie of London gentlemen (plus Lord Staines) to draw her into a dance under the nose of Thorne.

He laughed and joked with her, bestowing some shocking touches of gallantry, such as kissing her hand in an intimate way. As Cornelia joined her husband, they watched this little display, which Oriana responded to with feminine eyelash play, Thorne shot his wife a look of despair. Cornelia saw Grandiston's face freeze mid gallantry, looking over her shoulder. She turned. Clarissa had re-entered the ballroom.

Cornelia grasped her husband's sleeve, 'All is not lost,' she hissed.

Mr Thorne dropped his voice. 'Look how he is carrying on with Miss Petersham. I have a great regard for my sister, but no one could say she has the charms of her friend.'

'Nevertheless, look how he is prostrated by the sight of Clarissa. Whatever has occurred, all is not lost.'

John looked doubtfully at Grandiston, now laughing a little loudly with Oriana. 'I don't know ...'

'Well, I do. He is too forced. We must find out what precisely happened in the conservatory.'

'Miss Micklethwaite ...'

'She wouldn't tell me ... see if Booth knows what's wrong with his friend.'

'That's a bit tricky dearest ...'

'John.' Cornelia's tone changed.

'Going, my dear.'

Mr Elfoy was standing by a pillar with the prey as Thorne approached. 'Coming!' he hissed at Booth.

The Right Honourable Charles said in a stage whisper, with his back to Thorne, 'Grandiston's an idiot.'

Mr Elfoy came closer for the confidence and Thorne withdrew behind the pillar, hoping to hear what he could not respectfully ask.

'What occurred with Miss Thorne this evening? I thought he was *esprit* in that direction.'

'He is. We've all noticed it. Not his usual type either, which made me think that finally ...'

'We all thought so ...'

'But the problem is, Elfoy, that Grandiston has been so sought after that he must go slowly – he needs to be sure of her genuine attachment. And now Miss Thorne tells him that she's to depart with her brother in week or so ...'

'Well, he could still see her, couldn't he?'

'Of course. But you don't understand the man. He's not sure of himself as yet (even if all of us can see it as clear as a pikestaff) and to follow a girl into the country would encourage the world to think ...'

'Quite.'

'Bit of a libertine in his time, Grandiston. But he would never willingly offer such a slight to a lady. And then his pride ... he's not at all sure of her, either.' There was a pause. 'Juliana and I were hoping that with our staying at the Dower House, things could take their course over the summer.'

'But now he's diverting himself with Miss Petersham ...'

'Indeed - such a shame. I think Miss Thorne is just the girl for him.'

The two confidants wandered back towards the earl, to find a card room.

John Thorne, bristling with information, returned to his anxious wife.

CHAPTER 19

The Aftermath

At breakfast the next day, Cornelia was in high spirits. 'Such a night it was, my dear Clarissa, was it not?' She sipped at her chocolate and the ladies mistrusted the honeyed tones and the sweeter smile that accompanied them. 'Your engagement, my dearest Juliana, can only delight us all. And there was much more to be noted. All the London gentlemen danced with us. I declare it took me back to my giddy youth. And Mr Elfoy was so handsome last night, do you not agree, dear sister?' Here she looked at Clarissa keenly from below her lids. 'The whole ballroom is talking about how he led Annabel Challoner out to dance three times. A very marked attention.' Clarissa prevented herself from reacting - she had been tense enough to see him lead the vicar's daughter out twice, but must have been in the conservatory upon the third occasion.

'*Three* ...?' she breathed, but Miss Micklethwaite interrupted, 'Jam!' she said. Both ladies looked at her. 'I pray, Mrs Thorne, please pass the jam.' Cornelia did so gracelessly, turning back to her prey to assess her reaction. She suspected that Clarissa was closer to her agent than was decent or permissible. Grandiston could certainly elbow him out, but some estrangement certainly existed at the moment and there was no denying the agent was indecently handsome.

Clarissa had herself well in hand now and she merely said, 'That will give the gossips some fodder,' and she yawned, in the way any young lady might after the rigours of a ball.

'I believe that we must stay here for the summer after all, dearest sister. Whilst John is certain of a sale, it might be as well to enjoy the happy band of revellers for the near future.'

It seemed that the earl's ploy had worked. The ladies sighed as one.

Clarissa, in a mood of mischief, said plaintively, 'What a pity that I gave Lord Grandiston ... that is, Mr Booth, the news that their tenancy must be cut short. I believe the earl means to ...' her voice suspended on a sob, '... leave today.'

Cornelia left in haste to dispatch her husband (not yet risen) to the Dower House before his breakfast to forestall such a move.

'That,' said Juliana admiringly, 'was wicked. I didn't know that you had such a talent for dissembling.'

'I fear all of us have behaved most shamefully last evening,' Miss Appleby crooned, nibbling at a biscuit disinterestedly.

'The shame is that we needed a gentleman to pull it off.' Miss Micklethwaite looked at the assembled company. Juliana glowed, but the rest of the ladies were making efforts to cover up their moroseness. She guessed at the younger two. Oriana had been handed to their carriage by Grandiston and had continued her role with a flirtatious smile. The earl kissed her hand grandly and she had been scolded by Mrs Thorne all the way home for being fast. This was of course to plan, but the elder lady understood that Oriana's spirits had fallen when she reflected that the ruse was just that.

Mr Elfoy had handed Clarissa into the carriage but his touch was fleeting and cold and his manner unusually formal. He blamed Clarissa a little for the ruse, thought that it might become real and was realising the despair of his position. Clarissa just noticed his coldness and her spirit was frozen. Waity didn't blame her - there seemed to be no way of fixing that problem. It was too uneven a match.

This much Miss Micklethwaite understood, but why Louisa was so miserable, she could not at all guess.

Sullivan bent over the breakfast table to Clarissa, who roused herself at once. 'Might I have a word, Miss Clarissa?'

Clarissa gave him an intelligent look, roused from her torpor. She swept off to the library with Sullivan in her wake.

'First, Miss, there's a problem with Mrs Smith. Mrs Thorne will not surrender the keys to her and has issued orders that the housekeeper must apply to her if she wishes to unlock anything. Such an insult, Mrs Smith says, has not been offered to her in all her career. She wished to send word that she will accept no orders but yours, but I managed to stop that.'

'Oh thank you dear Sullivan. Until we think of a way to be rid of her, it is much better not to set up Mrs Thorne's back ...'

Clarissa was beginning to realise that an unconsidered result of last night's win was the continued presence of her brother and his wife. It was hard to bear. She needed to clear her head lest she let Cornelia have the black side of her tongue. She moved to the door, 'Ask Jed to bring around Sultan. I need to ride this morning before I encounter my sister-in-law once more.'

'Yes miss,' Sullivan coughed. 'There is one more thing I wish to bring to your attention ...'

But Clarissa was at the door. 'After my ride Sullivan,' she said much in the tone of her mother. 'And deny us to visitors this morning, except of course to the Dower House.' And she swept away. Sullivan debated following her, but decided against it. Instead he sent for Mr Elfoy as promised. But he feared that he may be too late.

Miss Appleby had, with difficulty, written her letters last night: one each to her three companions and another left on the hall table to be sent to Sir Montague. She felt, after all his kindness to her that she had better take her leave of him too and she enclosed a recipe for a reviving broth that she had discovered between the leaves of a book from the library. If only his cook could be encouraged to use it, perhaps his health might somewhat improve. On her last visit, he had taken a short walk in the garden with her and given her a rose with his own hands. She had preserved it between the pages of a book though she knew she was silly to do so. It was merely a gentlemanly gesture.

A gig had been ordered to come and collect her at eleven of the clock - it would take her to the stagecoach and then to her brother Farnham. She would arrive unannounced, it would be too dreadfully shaming, but quite her own fault for delaying her letter to her brother, as Mrs Thorne had let her know. No more simpering delays she had said, it would really be too selfish to soak off Clarissa for one more day. The gig would come to the servant's entrance. No one could intercept her. Mrs Thorne thought of everything.

Miss Micklethwaite tried her friend's door, but it was locked. She must be having a nap after their rollicking night at the ball. Appleby had danced with all the London gentlemen and had very likely exhausted herself. She would talk to her after luncheon.

Sullivan saw Miss Micklethwaite pass, and considered for a moment discussing the matter with her, but discretion is the watchword of a butler, and it was one thing to tell his mistress his suspicions, quite another to disseminate another lady's business further afield. Mr Elfoy had some foreknowledge and it was thus permissible to send him word, but further than this, Sullivan could not go. But he shook his head. The gig was already on its way.

Clarissa found that a rather longer ride than usual was necessary to clear her head. As she walked from the stables to the house, she felt that their victory of last night was hollow. The Thornes had their feet under the table in a way set fair to upend the household, including both staff and residents. Appleby had been distant this morning when she went to her room before breakfast; Juliana was living in a bubble of love that made empathy for the others' woes difficult; and to crown it all, Oriana seemed to suspect her of having designs on Grandiston. Dissembling had seemed quite fun at first, but in the cold light of day it was apparent that they would have to keep it up interminably and even then what would the end be? John would learn of the Grandiston deception and order her back to live with him. She could hardly bear it.

As she reached the house, it was to find a gentleman dismount from a fine but old-fashioned carriage. She tripped forward, guessing it to be Mr Sowersby, but instead found a gentleman dressed plainly in black with a venerable wig, also plain, upon his head.

'Mr Micklethwaite is it? How lovely to see you.'

'Miss Thorne, it is a pleasure to see you.' Micklethwaite, in stature very like his squat sister, bowed stiffly.

'Do come in, sir,' smiled Clarissa.

'I shall Miss Thorne, once I have directed the coachman to settle my bags at the inn.'

'You shall do no such thing, sir. You shall stay here tonight, of course.'

'It is an intrusion, I fear.'

'Not at all. Your sister has set about the organisation of this house so that it is quite simple to accommodate you. We do not want for rooms as you see.' She moved her hand to indicate the vast sprawl of the house.

They mounted the stairs to the imposing front doors as they talked comfortably.

'Your sister will be so pleased.'

Micklethwaite smiled a little dolefully. 'I might not have come, but for her requesting information on a little legal matter regarding your present situation. It is a rather complex reply, so that I thought it better to come here myself.'

'How kind,' - but Clarissa said this absently, for Mr Elfoy was galloping down the drive, his horse's flanks lathered.

He dropped to the ground handing the reins to Mr Micklethwaite's bemused groom and started up the steps two at a time.

Meanwhile, Oriana was walking in the garden, determined to avoid Cornelia, Thorne and any morning callers. It was wonderful that their ruse had worked but she too had suddenly realised the precariousness of their position. Grandiston and Clarissa had played their parts well last night, she could almost believe that the earl had feelings for her friend and as much as Oriana knew that Clarissa favoured Mr Elfoy, she understood that this connection would not be permitted by Clarissa's brother. It would be seven years until Clarissa attained her majority and it was useless to suppose that last night's play could do more than delay the inevitable. Grandiston genuinely liked Clarissa and had paid only cursory attention to her before last night's performance. Perhaps this thing he had with her friend would prosper and it was not for her to stand in his way.

But when they had danced it was like old times. But no, it was better. For in those blind days, Oriana had not known how much she loved and admired her father's teasing companion. She knew he was handsome and funny and annoying, but she had not known then that there was no man to rival him – not one of her suitors had come near to the excitement that his presence instilled in her.

She had directed her steps to the back of the house to avoid detection and now was confronted by several workmen lowering slate from the roof in a sacking sling and then loading it onto a waiting cart. Most of them wore a relic of army uniform, some the trousers and another a tattered jacket and she stood for a minute or two and watched them, noting a damaged hand on one man that necessitated that another man with a limp had to load him up with the slate bag so that he could carry it. Oriana, standing by a tree so as not to interrupt, had tears in her eyes. These were the brave soldiers who had routed Napoleon, still bravely overcoming their woes. Oriana felt ashamed - what troubles did she have that could compare? Perhaps she would end up living with Fitzroy again but it would not at all matter, she thought miserably.

From the Dower House path came the sound of a horse: Grandiston had dismounted before she had time to avoid him.

'Well met. How did our scheme prosper?' he said, noting the lowness of her mood.

'Surely Mr Thorne called on you this morning to apprise you?'

'Before breakfast? I denied myself. He left a message to be sure to call when I arose. I rode over as soon as my neckcloth was tied to my valet's satisfaction. He's a bit of a stickler, you know.' Oriana gave a wan smile. 'The young lover and his future in-laws walked over at an untimely hour. What does Thorne want with me?'

In a dull voice, Oriana said, 'Mrs Thorne has relented. We are all to stay for the summer.'

'Hah!' said the earl with satisfaction.

Oriana turned her startling blue eyes upon him – less glacier and more stormy sea. 'That's all very well, but she and Thorne are staying too. It will cut up all our peace.'

She was glad to see Grandiston's face lose its smugness. 'Surely she will need to return to her children?'

Oriana just looked.

'An affectionate mother indeed.' Still with the reins in his hands, Grandiston sat on a log and offered his coattails for Oriana to join him. She sat without restraint, her annoyance with him putting her back into their old relations. 'Well, we shall just have to get rid of them,' he said decidedly.

'Good for us. How shall we achieve it? You could offer for Clarissa, I suppose,' she said in a voice of affected nonchalance, 'and that might leave Cornelia free to go home to inform all her acquaintance. She'd want to see their faces as she dropped the news.'

'Indeed. And shall we plan the wedding as well?'

Oriana stiffened, 'It seems you like her well enough. And you are getting no younger, Grandiston. Clarissa would make a wonderful wife.'

'She would.' For a second, Oriana turned those stormy eyes on him then returned to her stiffened posture, clutching her hands together. 'But I fear I may be dead within the week,' he continued musingly, 'Elfoy and I went hunting the other day. He's a crack shot. And then ...' Oriana found herself weakening at the laugh in his voice, but she dared not turn around until he said, '... your father meant *you* for me.' His eyes were shining down on her; his harsh face alight with laughter and a deeper warmth that made her shiver.

'And are you so obedient to my father's will?' she asked, trembling, but bristling too.

His strong arms snaked around her, turning her shoulders towards him. 'No, my darling, but when I was away I could not forget my little fighting cock. I could never stop thinking of you Oriana.' His face was serious now and he bent to kiss her and she found herself responding with a sudden heat. For just ten seconds they were locked together and his ardour frightened her. She jerked away and almost without her will delivered herself of a full strength slap on his face. He reeled then got to his feet, and pulled her back into his arms.

'You firebrand! What was that for?'

'How could you believe I ever agreed to that dreadful engagement?'

'I only believed it for a moment. I assumed it was one of your hot-headed tricks to escape your brother and that you repented before too long.' This was not the full truth, but Grandiston would not tell her of the doubts he had harboured for such a short time. As soon as he had met her again, he realised that not even her youth could have lowered her pride enough to bear such an engagement and he saw how Petersham had been at fault. For which he would, assuredly, pay.

'No, my hot-headed trick was to answer an advert for a school mistress in Mrs Thorne's School for Young Ladies.' She sighed, relaxing against his shoulder. 'Oh Grandiston, I love you most dreadfully.'

'Well, don't sound so miserable about it.' He kissed her again.

'It is just that you will seek to rule me just as much as Fitzroy and I couldn't bear it.'

Grandiston rubbed his jaw where she had slapped him. 'I shall be much too afraid to do any such thing. I shall tremble whenever I see your eyes turn that fascinating colour and shall resort to answering each of your requests with 'Certainly my love' just as John Thorne does.'

He had tucked her hand in the crook of his arm and was leading her towards the path, aware that lingering with a gentleman in the woods was not at all the thing for his lady's reputation. They had a little way to go and Oriana looked up at him shyly, quite unlike herself. 'Are we engaged then?' She blushed – this was not a permissible question.

Grandiston laughed. 'I should hope so. I have your engagement gift at home. Bought it in Biddulf's before I arrived.'

Oriana recognised the name of a smart London jeweller. 'You have meant to propose since before you arrived?' She stopped dead, her eyes a blue storm once more.

Grandiston gave a crack of laughter. 'I should think you would be pleased at my constancy sweetheart.'

She pulled away. 'Don't you "sweetheart" me, Grandiston. When I think how you have played hot and cold with me all this time ...'

He pulled her once more into his arms and she gave weak resistance. 'I wanted to be as sure of you as I was of myself, darling, darling girl. And I must admit, when I saw the way you froze all those others, I was too afraid. They walked away wounded to a man.'

She hit at him with her small fists, but she was too happy to resist his laughter. 'Oh my love ...' They were in sight of the front of the house now. Grandiston denied her the kiss she leaned in for and tucked her hand in her arm again, whilst a large coach came bowling along the drive at fast pace dashing past them.

'What the devil?'

'Whose coach was that?'

They picked up their pace and hurried to the house.

In the distance another vehicle, the vicar's pony and trap, was sedately going towards the house, whilst three gentlemen on horseback passed it, going in the same direction.

Oriana turned, seeing the horsemen in the distance. 'Oh Grandiston, where on earth can I hide?'

He held her elbow. 'Oh, no you don't. Remember Clarissa. I have a suspicion that this farce is coming to an end quite soon.'

Oriana sighed. 'Clarissa. Of course. But don't look at me Hugo, or I fear I shall not be able to disguise how happy I am.' She turned back towards the house and entered the hall to find an unusual number of persons gathered there.

CHAPTER 20

The Denoument

Clarissa had entered the Great Hall with her guest and visitor. Elfoy said, 'I must speak to you.'

'Certainly - in a moment. Mr Micklethwaite, this is my agent, Mr Elfoy.' The gentlemen exchanged slight bows. 'Sullivan, could you tell Miss Micklethwaite that her brother has arrived?'

Sullivan bowed, but said in an under-voice, 'I believe Mr Elfoy is here on an urgent matter.'

The doorbell rang and Clarissa turned to Elfoy after an apologetic look at Micklethwaite who gestured his patience.

'Is she still here?' he asked in a lowered voice.

'Who on earth ...?'

'Hasn't Sullivan told you?'

'I've been out.' She was distracted by the sight of a wheezing Sir Montague Holmes entering the house on the arm of an attendant.

'Has she gone?' coughed the baronet.

'We don't yet know.'

Clarissa was beginning to guess. 'Appleby? Oh, no. Sullivan ...'

'Miss Appleby left in a gig from the village a half hour ago. I tried to tell you before your ride that the gig had been summoned.' Sullivan coughed discreetly.

A loud voice from the direction of the kitchen stairs interrupted. 'Clarissa, I must insist that you dispatch this woman from your service. She has been insolent in the extreme. Never have I ...' Cornelia came into view marching indignantly, followed by Mrs Smith, Becky, and two of the village girls who worked in the kitchens. This cortege stopped when Cornelia did. Discomfited to see the visitors, she drew breath to greet them. Mrs Smith seized her advantage and swept past her towards her mistress.

Had she had leisure to notice, Clarissa would have seen that Mrs Smith, every bit as stiff and upright with indignation as Cornelia, was looking the healthiest she had been for a long time. Rage had put colour in her cheeks and a sparkle in her eye. 'I hope you know, Miss Clarissa, that I have not been insolent to my betters once in my career. I only informed Miss Thorne that I was not about to surrender the key to the silver cabinet to any but my mistress.'

Clarissa's head was reeling and she could only think of dear Appleby, but she must clear the servants away first.

'I understand, Mrs Smith; not now if you please, we'll sort this out later.'

'Yes – take yourself off,' ordered Cornelia, recovering herself.

'What's the commotion?' Charles, Juliana and the Sowersbys came out of the breakfast room at the same time as Grandiston pushed open the front door and entered with Oriana.

Clarissa went towards her. 'Appleby's gone.'

Oriana met her and grasped her shaking hands, 'But how, why?'

Sir Montague grabbed onto Grandiston's arm. 'She sent me a letter. Thought I might catch her ...'

The earl pulled forward a chair. 'Calm yourself, sir. Sit.'

'Damned legs!' said the baronet, and stretched them out. He looked up at Grandiston, 'I should have spoken more clearly to her.' The other man's hand grasped his shoulder.

Meanwhile Mr Elfoy was pacing. 'The poor lady - I knew of her plans before but I persuaded her to delay until after the ball. I didn't think she'd leave the day after.'

'Why did you not tell me?' said Clarissa. 'Oh, let me think ... why would she?'

'Because,' said the stentorian voice of Miss Micklethwaite descending the staircase, clutching a note, 'Mrs Thorne told her to go.'

John Thorne, attracted by the sounds, like Booth and company, followed her down the stairs and overtook her to stand beside his wife and grasp her shoulder comfortingly. 'You have no right to accuse my wife of such a thing,' he said courageously, looking up at his childhood bête noir, 'I will not stand by and ...'

Lord Grandiston interrupted. 'Sullivan, who ordered the carriage to take Miss Appleby to the stagecoach?'

Sullivan, who had been directing the kitchen boy to make himself useful and take Mr Micklethwaite's bags up the back stairs, said passionlessly, 'Mrs Thorne, your Lordship.'

Mrs Thorne found all eyes upon her whilst her husband said, 'But Miss Appleby ...'

Cornelia's cheeks were a little flushed, but she turned towards her husband. 'We were agreed that these poor relations could not batten on our dear sister forever.'

John looked genuinely shocked. 'Well, yes. But she would have left when Clarissa came home with us – not alone.'

His wife turned to address the others. 'I have nothing to reproach myself with - Miss Appleby saw that it would be wrong to stay here any longer, sponging off Clarissa.'

Mr Elfoy could stand it no longer. 'If you had any idea what Miss Appleby has done for Ashcroft; what all the ladies have done. Her organisation of the glasshouses alone will help feed the house and many others too. She has helped Miss Thorne tend the sick on the estate, organise the house, set the linen to rights, train the servants, and work out the finer rules of etiquette for dealing with so many. And more than that, she has helped the best landlord this estate has had in many years adjust to her life as the lady of the manor, and did this all simply out of her affectionate heart.'

Clarissa placed a hand on her chest which swelled with pride. Mr Elfoy stood facing Cornelia across the hall, his curly locks falling over one eye.

'That's telling her!' said Booth in a stage whisper to his party. Mrs Thorne winced.

Clarissa moved forward to grasp Mr Elfoy's hands passionately. 'Could you not go after the stage - might we catch her still?'

Elfoy grasped her hands and looked passionately down at her, 'I only delayed in case she should still be here ...'

'That's it boy,' Lord Montague encouraged from his seat behind, 'get going.'

At the same moment Thorne's outraged voice rang out. 'Clarissa. How dare you?'

The couple sprang apart. The doorbell rang.

'Sullivan, deny us.'

Reflecting that they had better move out of the hall if they wished to be denied, Sullivan opened the door a little then said with undiminished solemnity, 'The ladies are not at home.' The gentlemen left their cards, although Clarissa heard Sir Piers' voice sounding a little put out.

'Perhaps we are too early. We shall call later.'

'As you wish sir.'

The sounds of the gentlemen departed, and the crowd in the hall breathed as one. Before they could resume talking, the door sounded again and Sullivan opened it a little, then pulled it back. In walked Mr Elfoy's mother supporting a distressed Miss Appleby, who seemed to be having the vapours.

Clarissa ran forward and threw her arms around her friend, 'Darling Appleby!' The rest of the ladies were hardly a beat behind her and Miss Appleby was hidden in the throng.

Mrs Elfoy moved towards her son, smiling. 'The landlord at the inn sent for me since Miss Appleby was in rather a state. She had been crying ever since she got in the gig apparently, and when she reached the inn she was so much overcome that the stagecoach driver would not consent to sell her a ticket. I resolved to bring her home.'

Sir Montague struggled to his feet, 'Dear lady,' he said, regarding Miss Appleby, his handkerchief dabbing at his eyes, 'dear lady.'

The calm voice of Mrs Sowersby, still standing with her family by the door of the blue salon intoned, 'Now that Miss Appleby is found, would it not be better to retire to somewhere a little more comfortable to continue this?'

But Cornelia moved forward to the centre of the hall, whilst Sir Montague aided Miss Appleby, smiling through her sobs, to his seat. Grandiston, with the silent spirit of Sullivan, had already placed another beside it onto which the baronet gratefully sank. Oriana smiled at the earl and moved to his side without thinking. Cornelia's fulminating eyes took it all in.

'After that disgraceful show, Clarissa, it is obvious to me where your affections lie.' Clarissa turned full towards her, glancing over at Elfoy briefly, but he had turned his head lest he betray himself. She held her ground and looked her sister-in-law in the eye, but couldn't say anything.

John Thorne came to join his wife. 'I don't understand. Do you not favour Lord Grandiston?'

Grandiston tucked Oriana's hand in his arm and sauntered forward. 'Doesn't matter if she does, I'm afraid. I'm going to marry Miss Petersham.'

'Oh, wonderful!' 'Congratulations!' 'You're a dark horse!' said Clarissa, Miss Micklethwaite and Mr Booth simultaneously.

Miss Appleby had stopped sobbing. 'Oh, did you hear it sir? Oriana will be a Countess.'

Sir Montague kissed the little hand he had been patting. 'Not before I make you a Lady, my dear. These youngsters have time to wait.'

Only Miss Micklethwaite, standing by her chair heard the gruff old man make his plea. With a squeeze of Louisa's shoulder, she moved across the hall to her brother.

Miss Appleby found that she could not talk. Instead, she let out a sigh that was so long that it let go all the disappointments of her past and she lifted his hand to her cheek, dropping her head and resting it there as an answer.

Cornelia was beside herself with rage. 'It is my belief this whole thing was just some plot made up by you and your sponging attendants ...'

'Madame!' began Mr Micklethwaite, outraged for his sister's sake.

'... to enable you to stay on your great estate until all the money is gone and you are once more a pauper. And *then* you'll come begging to your brother.' She paused, but Clarissa did not speak. 'I'll wager you have very little of the legacy from your mother left.'

Clarissa flinched. The ladies did not know how close she was to having used up her mother's bequest. 'And on top of this you wish to marry a man who doesn't have two shillings to rub together to support you and will just be yet another hard luck story designed to part you from your wealth.'

A gasp ran around the room. Cornelia's rage had spilled over dangerously. She had insulted half the room. 'I have always said,' Mr Sowersby whispered loudly to Mrs Elfoy, leading her towards his group by the salon, 'that Mrs Thorne is a dashed unpleasant person.'

Cornelia had shocked herself and now she was quiet.

'What my wife is trying to say, sister, though I admit her concern for you has led her to speak a little heatedly, is that any unequal match is not to be thought of and that rather than wasting your time at Ashcroft any more, you must return with us for your own protection.'

'He's said it. The very words we've all been dreading,' Miss Micklethwaite said aside to her brother. 'The jig is up. I suppose you've come to take me home with you.'

'Not quite. There is another errand I must perform,' he returned.

'You speak of an unequal match,' said the languid tone of Grandiston, leaning against the bannister, 'but I don't think it so. Mr Elfoy's family is just as ancient as Miss Thorne's. The stumbling block is of course, the means.'

Clarissa gave a tiny squeal. 'Would everyone stop talking about a match? Mr Elfoy has never even asked me to dance, never mind marry him.'

Booth slapped Elfoy on the back, 'That's because of the dratted mullah. If he was the gold digger you think him, Thorne, he'd have stopped just drooling over Clarissa and proposed long ago.'

Thorne looked daggers at Booth.

'Or accepted when she proposed to him,' offered Miss Micklethwaite.

'Clarissa!' John's outrage was close to causing him to burst a button on his handsome waistcoat.

'*He* doesn't drool - I'm the one who pines. It's not his fault at all.'

Elfoy, who had been avoiding Clarissa's eye since the hand clasp had shaken him, now turned to her fully, catching her gaze. 'I do drool. Often.' His voice held a laugh and she smiled back at him. 'I didn't know if you did. You seemed to enjoy his Lordship's company so much.' His voice was soft, intimate.

'Grandiston? He's old enough to be my ...'

'Uncle,' Grandiston interrupted suavely. 'The money ... Once upon a time, Thorne, this estate was a rich one indeed. And in perhaps three or more years, it can be again. There will be more cultivation, more habitable cottages for the workers, and this will lead to more rents. It will take hard work, creativity, passion and knowhow. Miss Thorne can supply her share of the first three, but it'll take Elfoy to supply the latter.' John Thorne wore a stubborn look. 'Would it really be better having Clarissa with you?' Grandiston's tone changed to his old familiar one, '... a happy home is contentment for life and I think it is safe to say that your sister and your wife will often be at each other's throats. Do you really wish to live amongst that?' He moved and put his hand under Cornelia's chin tipping it up. 'And you Mrs Thorne. Think of the house parties that you can tell your friends about. I'll bet there are few of your acquaintance who will be able to boast a sister with a home of this size to visit. Not to forget the other guests. Why, when next you visit London, you'll be invited everywhere, I'll wager.'

John Thorne stepped forward doggedly. 'You make a strong argument, my lord, but *I* am still Clarissa's guardian. And after the way my sister has deceived us I have no confidence in her judgement or her ability to make this wealthy estate you speak of. My sister needs moral guidance, whatever the sacrifice to my home life.'

'John ...' protested Cornelia, for Grandiston's vision had drawn a pretty picture in her head.

'No my dear, I am her guardian and I forbid it,' John said stoutly.

There was a deathly pause. Clarissa found Elfoy's hand and clasped it tightly in the folds of her dress. Her eyes filled.

Mr Micklethwaite gave a cough. 'I'm afraid that isn't so ...' he said apologetically.

'I beg your pardon, sir?'

'Well, Mr Tipperton - the solicitor for the Ashcroft family - had the right, as executor of Mrs Thorne's estate, to appoint a guardian. As the elder brother, he of course believed it would be you, Mr Thorne and I believe he wrote to you after your stepmother's death asking you when Miss Thorne would be residing under your roof.'

John squirmed. 'She was happy at the school at the time and my wife was quite unwell ...'

'Yes, indeed. And according to my sister it was not until she inherited Ashcroft, a full year later, that the invitation to reside with you was offered.'

John Thorne was looking discomfited, unable to meet any of the many eyes that regarded him. 'The school was no longer profitable, it is not as simple as you suggest.'

'However that may be, in order to give Miss Thorne her mother's portion, Tipperton appointed another guardian - himself. It was even more necessary after the young viscount died. Mr Tipperton is getting old and he has now appointed another legal man as guardian ...' He coughed again. '... me.'

A gasp of wonder went around the room and Mr Mickleth-waite, embarrassed at being the centre of attention stepped back a pace.

'Do you mean to say,' declared The Honourable Charles disgustedly, 'That all our carefully thought out stratagems for outwitting Clarissa's guardian, not forgetting that whole charade last night was all for nothing? All we need have done is to have applied to Waity's brother?'

'As to that sir, I am only lately, after receipt of my sister's inquiry, appointed by Mr Tipperton. He was looking about him, you see, for someone he could depend on and when I explained my sister's connection ... but you only need have applied to Mr Tipperton, certainly.'

'I do not at all understand. How is it I did not know about Mr Tipperton's guardianship?' asked Clarissa.

The weak voice of Miss Appleby, situated behind Clarissa, sounded out, 'I'm afraid that might have been my fault, my dear Clarissa.'

'How so, dear Appleby?' asked Clarissa, turning to her.

'Well, there were a deal of papers sent quite soon after your mother's death. Mostly Augusta dealt with them, but one arrived when you and she were walking and I put it behind the clock and there it stayed for some months. When we packed to go, I found it once more and put it in my valise, meaning to give it to you when we arrived.' She sighed. 'But what with one thing or another ... I'm *so* sorry, my dear.'

'Do you mean to say that I had to endure those awful morning visits and even smile once at Lord Staines for *nothing*. How infamous,' said Miss Petersham severely.

Clarissa laughed. 'You did it for friendship, Oriana. And oh, has anyone ever had such wonderful friends? Waity and Appleby and Oriana, my three treasures - and then our new friends: Grandiston, Mr Booth and dear Sir Montague. And Mr Elfoy, who stood up to everyone and anyone to help me. How can I ever thank you?' She turned with her old impetuosity and clasped his hands once more.

Elfoy searched her eyes. 'By marrying me?'

Clarissa glowed, for once devoid of speech. Mrs Elfoy grasped Mr Somersby's arm hard enough to make him gasp. Elfoy turned to Mr Micklethwaite. 'With your permission, sir.'

'Given Lord Grandiston's masterly summation of the facts, I should think that it will be a very sensible conclusion.'

Mr Elfoy stood gazing into his beloved's eyes, Grandiston looked with pride on the face of Oriana, the joy in it doubled by her happiness for her friend. Sir Montague was still patting Miss Appleby's hand and whispering softly to her. The rest of the company were in various states of shock, so it fell to Mrs Sowersby to move things along.

'Mr Elfoy, perhaps it would be better if you took Clarissa for a walk in the garden.'

'Yes, ma'am,' he said with alacrity.

'And don't talk to her about your lack of money. Charles and Hugo tell me you are worth ten thousand a year to this place.'

'No ma'am.' Elfoy smiled and joyfully led Miss Thorne into the garden.

'We'll leave the other lovers to sort themselves out, but I suggest the rest of us adjurn to the salon to escape the draught. That includes you and Charles, Juliana. You have been engaged a full day now and can have no more need for quiet cozes.' She smiled radiantly and turned to the butler. 'Sullivan, is it? Do you think we might manage some refreshments? It's been far too exciting this morning.'

Sullivan bowed magnificently and sailed away. Out of sight, he smiled widely. His little Miss Clarissa was safe. But the house and garden needed a great deal more staff. Once the men had finished with the cottages, he'd put them to work elsewhere. Ashcroft would one day be great again.

Mrs Sowersby ushered Mrs Elfoy and Mr and Miss Micklethwaite ahead of her family and looked back at the Thornes standing stock still and embarrassed by the grand staircase. 'Dear Mrs. Thorne, it has been an exciting morning and I suppose like me you will be craving tea.' Cornelia hesitated but seeing nothing but kindness in the face of her most illustrious neighbour, she walked forward tentatively. 'Your sister is getting married. I'm sure upon reflection that you see it is right,' Mrs Sowersby continued companionably as she led her forward. 'I suspect Miss Appleby's wedding will take place from here and soon.' Mrs Thorne's face froze. 'But we too have weddings to arrange, dear lady.' With the others gliding through the salon doors, she turned back to Grandiston still standing with Miss Petersham's arm through his, gazing down at her. 'What do you say, my Lord, shall we plan a triple wedding? I daresay society will never have seen the like.'

'I leave the conspiracies all to you, Mrs Sowersby,' he said in his old suave manner, 'Miss Petersham and I intend to be married by special license – *immediately.*'

'But Grandiston ...' protested Oriana.

'Do you *want* your brother at your wedding?'

'Immediately it is, Hugo.' Oriana answered, revolted by the thought. 'But if you think you can rule me ...'

He dragged her out the door, past the gentle lovers seated in the hall, and looked to see a private path.

That evening the table had to have nearly all its leaves put on and the cook had excelled herself in presenting many excellent dishes (with the help of three extra girls from the village).

'Well,' said Clarissa, 'so it is settled. Miss Micklethwaite will remain here and live with us. So sorry, Mr Micklethwaite.'

Mr Micklethwaite gave another dry cough and his sister said, equally dryly, 'I believe he will survive. Though Mr Elfoy may not.'

Elfoy smiled. 'Well, I tried to get Clarissa to change her mind ...'

Micklethwaite rapped him with her fork. 'At least I shall have your mother to bear me company.' She exchanged smiles with Mrs Elfoy.

'And Miss Appleby will be with us until spring when she will become Lady Holmes and be much too grand for us.'

Miss Appleby blushed and Sir Montague barked a laugh. 'We shall go to London to Ashcroft House before I have to sell it for next year's wages.'

'I suggest you lease it, my dear,' chipped in Sir Montague. 'It's a damned good address. It could realise a goodly sum.'

'How clever you are, Sir Montague. I depend upon many visits.' She smiled brightly, then continued, 'Juliana and I will have a quiet double wedding ...'

'We'll see about that. My wife has other plans,' said Mr Sowersby matter-of-factly.

'... attended by The Earl and Countess of Grandiston which will make us all madly fashionable.'

Grandiston cast an eye over Booth's snazzy brocade waistcoat, 'If you continue to dress like that Charles, even I cannot help you.'

'Quiet Grandiston,' said Clarissa, 'Or should I say My Lord?' she looked to Miss Appleby for guidance.

'Yes my dear,' said that lady, 'But whatever you call him, I'm perfectly sure you shouldn't tell an earl to be quiet.'

John Thorne looked like he would have given solid agreement to this, but he was quashed by his wife's arm. Cornelia was lying low. Much social advancement now lay in Clarissa's gift. Her resentment was quelled beneath practical concerns. They must not be cut out of the wedding.

'It's only Grandiston. And he was *my* suitor until last night you know,' she said naughtily.

'But *thank goodness* you are now engaged to someone else,' Grandiston said with heavy relief and raised a glass to Elfoy, who grinned.

'I always thought earls would have better manners,' Clarissa admonished him. She stood and raised her glass, surveying her friends and her kingdom which no longer seemed so daunting. 'I have a toast: to poor relations everywhere! May they find a life as full, happy and useful as all of us!'

Also By Alicia Cameron

Regency Romance

Angelique and the Pursuit of Destiny: getbook.at/Angelique

Angelique was named by her French grandmother, but now lives as Ann, ignored by her aristocratic relations. Can she find the courage to pursue her Destiny, reluctantly aided by her suave cousin Ferdinand?

Beth and the Mistaken Identity: getbook.at/Beth

Beth has been cast off as lady's maid to the pert young Sophy Ludgate, but is mistaken as a lady herself by a handsome marquis and his princess sister. Desperate to save the coach fare to London, she goes along with them, but they do not let her escape so easily.

Clarissa and the Poor Relations: getbook.at/Clarissa
Clarissa Thorne and her three friends have to leave their cosy School for Young Ladies after the death of Clarissa's mama. all must be sent off as poor relations to their families. However, Clarissa suddenly inherits Ashcroft Manor, and persuades the ladies to make a bid for freedom. But can she escape their unpleasant families? The Earl of Grandiston might help.

Delphine and the Dangerous Arrangement: getbook.at/Delphine
Delphine Delacroix was brought up by her mother alone, a cold and unloving childhood. With her mother dead, she has become the richest young lady in England, and is taken under the wing of her three aunts, Not quite trusting them, Delphine enters a dangerous arrangement with the handsome Viscount Gascoigne - but will this lead to her downfall?

The Fentons Series (Regency)

Honoria and the Family Obligation, The Fentons 1
https://getbook.at/Honoria
Honoria Fenton has been informed that the famous Mr Allison is to come to her home. His purpose? To woo her. She cannot recall what he looks like, since he made

her nervous when they met in Town. Her sister Serena is amused, but when Allison arrives, it seems that a mistake might cost all three there happiness.

Felicity and the Damaged Reputation, The Fentons 2
https://getbook.at/Felicity
On her way to London to take a post as governess, Felicity Oldfield is intercepted by xx, who asks her to impersonate his cousin for an hour. When, in an unexpected turn of events, Felicity is able to enjoy a London Season, this encounter damages her reputation.

Euphemia and the Unexpected Enchantment, The Fentons 3 https://getbook.at/Euphemia
Euphemia, plain and near forty, is on her way to live with her dear friend Felicity and her husband when she is diverted to the home of Baron x, a bear of a man as huge and loud as Euphemia is small and quiet. Everything in her timid life begins to change.

Ianthe and the Fighting Foxes: The Fentons 4 https://getbook.at/Ianthe
The Fighting Foxes, Lord Edward, his half-brother Curtis and Lady Fox, his stepmother, are awaiting the arrival from France of a poor relation, Miss Ianthe Eames. But when Ianthe turns up, nothing could be further from their idea of a supplicant. Richly dressed and in high good humour, Ianthe takes the Foxes by storm.

The Sisters of Castle Fortune Series (Regency)

Georgette and the Unrequited Love: Sisters of Castle Fortune 1 https://getbook.at/Georgette

Georgette Fortune, one of ten sisters, lives as a spinster in Castle Fortune. She refused all offers during her London Seasons, since she fell in love, at first glance with the dashing Lord Onslow. He hardly knew she existed, however, but now he has arrived at the castle for a house party, and Georgette is fearful of exposing her feelings. She tries to avoid him, but Onslow treats her as a friend, making Georgette's pain worse, even as he makes her laugh.

Jocasta and the Cruelty of Kindness: Sisters of Castle Fortune 2 https://getbook.at/Jocasta

At a house party in Castle Fortune, Jocasta's beau had fallen for her sister, Portia. Now Jocasta is back in London and has to suffer the pity of the friends and family that care for her. Only Sir Damon Regis treats her without pity, and she is strangely drawn to him because of it.

Katerina and the Reclusive Earl: Sisters of Castle Fortune 3

Katerina Fortune has only one desire, to avoid going on her London Season altogether. On the journey, she hears of a recluse, who dislikes people as much as she. Katerina escapes her father and drives to offer a convenient marriage to the earl, who refuses. But an accident

necessitates her stay at his home, and they discover they have more in common than either could have believed.

Leonora and the Lion's Venture: Sisters of Castle Fortune 4

At the Castle Fortune house party three years ago, fourteen year-old Leonora fell out of a tree and into the arms of the the shy Mr Linton Carswell. From that minute on she decided to wed him and secretly prepared herself to be a good wife. Leonora's goals are known as the Lion's Ventures to her sisters, but although the know she has a new venture, not even her twin Marguerite knows what it is precisely. But when the lovely twins arrive in London, they begin to realise her unlikely target. Foggy Carswell, not a marrying man, begins to suspect too and hides from his pursuer. But Leonora, the most determined of her sisters, is set on him. But when she sets him free at last, the tables finally turn.

Edwardian Inspirational Romance

(typewriters, bicycles, and leg-of-mutton sleeves!)

Francine and the Art of Transformation: get-book.at/FrancineT

Francine is fired as a lady's maid, but she is a woman who has planned for every eventuality. Meeting Miss Philpott, a timid, unemployed governess, Francine

transforms her into the Fascinating Mathilde and offers her another, self directed life. Together, they help countless other women get control over their lives.

Francine and the Winter's Gift: getbook.at/FrancineW
Francine and Mathilde continue to save young girls from dreadful marriages, while seeing to their own romances. In Francine, Sir Hugo Portas, government minister, meets a woman he could never have imagined. Will society's rules stop their union, or can Francine even accept the shackles of being in a relationship?

About Author

Alicia Cameron lives between her homes in rural Scotland and rural France. She reads avidly, laughs a lot, and is newly addicted, unfortunately, to Korean Dramas ... for which she refuses treatment. Here is a link to get **Angelique and the Pursuit of Destiny** for FREE! https://BookHip.com/XSNQ VM It puts you on the list to receive Alicia Cameron's book news and offers, occasionally. You can find the link on the first page of Alicia Cameron's website, too! It has news of new books and there is also an occasional Regency Blog.

All Alicia books are available on Amazon and as audiobooks on Audible. Some are available in several languages, German and Spanish especially.

You can find out more here :

The website https://aliciacameron.co.uk

Facebook https://www.facebook.com/alicia-cameron.100

Twitter https://twitter.com/aliciaclarissa2

Bookbub https://www.bookbub.com/authors/alicia-cameron

A Chapter of the first book in the Fentons Series to tempt you....

Honoria and the Family Obligation

The Fentons Book 1

Alicia Cameron

Getbook.at/Honoria

Blue Slippers

'He has arrived!' said Serena, kneeling on the window seat of their bedchamber. She made a pretty picture there with her sprigged muslin dress foaming around her and one silk stockinged foot still on the floor, but her sister Honoria was too frozen with fear to notice.

'Oh, no,' said Honoria, moving forward in a dull fashion to join her. Her elder brother Benedict had been sitting with one leg draped negligently over the arm of the only comfortable chair in the room and now rose languidly to join his younger sisters. After the season in London, Dickie had begun to ape the manners of Beau Brummel and his cronies, polite, but slightly bored with the world. At one and twenty, it seemed a trifle contrived, even allowing that his long limbs and handsome face put many a town beau to shame.

Serena's dark eyes danced wickedly, 'Here comes the conquest of your triumphant season, your soon-to-be-fiancé.'

Dickie grinned, rather more like their childhood companion, 'Your knight in shining armour. If *only* you could remember him.'

'It isn't funny.'

Serena laughed and turned back to the window as she heard the door of the carriage open and the steps let down by Timothy, the one and only footman that Fenton Manor could boast.

'Oh, how did it happen?' Honoria said for the fifteenth time that morning.

Someone in the crowd had said, 'Mr Allison is approaching. But he never dances!' In confusion, she had looked around, and saw the throng around her grow still and part as her hostess approached with a tall gentleman. With all eyes turned to her she stiffened in every sinew. She remembered the voice of Lady Carlisle introducing Mr Allison as a desirable partner, she remembered her mother thrusting her forward as she was frozen with timidity. She remembered his hand lead her to her first waltz of the season. She had turned to her mother for protection as his hand snaked around her waist and had seen that matron grip her hands together and glow with pride. This was Lady Fenton's shining moment, if not her daughter's. Word had it that Mr Allison had danced only thrice this season, each time with his married friends. Lost in the whirl of the dance, she had answered his remarks with single syllables, looking no higher than his chin. A dimpled chin, strong, she remembered vaguely. And though she had previously seen Mr. Allison at a distance, the very rich and therefore very interesting Mr Allison, with an estate grander than many a nobleman, she could not remember more than that he was held to be handsome. (As she told Serena this later, her sister remarked that rich men were very often held to be handsome, strangely related to the size of their purse.)

There was the waltz; there had been a visit to her father in the London house; her mother had informed her of Mr Allison's wishes and that she was to receive his addresses the next afternoon. He certainly visited the next afternoon, and Honoria had been suffered to serve him his tea and her hand had shaken so much that she had kept her eyes on the cup for the rest of the time. He had not proposed, which her mother thought of as a pity, but here she had been saved by Papa, who had thought that Mr Allison should visit them in the country where his daughter and he might be more at their leisure to know each other. 'For she is a little shy with new company and I should wish her perfectly comfortable before she receives your addresses,' Sir Ranalph had told him, as Honoria's mama had explained.

Serena, when told, had thought it a wonderful joke. To be practically engaged to someone you could not remember! She laughed because she trusted to good-natured Papa to save Honoria from the match if it should prove unwanted; her sister had only to say "no".

'Why on earth do you make such a tragedian of yourself, Orry,' had said Serena once Honoria had poured her story out, 'After poor Henrietta Madeley's sad marriage, Papa has always said that to marry with such parental compulsion is scandalously cruel.'

And Honoria had mopped up her tears and felt a good deal better, buoyed by Serena's strength of mind. To be sure, there was the embarrassment to be endured of giving disappointment, but she resolved to do it if Mr Allison's aura of grandeur continued to terrify her.

'And then,' her sister had continued merrily, 'the rich Mr Allison may just turn out to be as handsome as his purse and as good natured as Papa - and you will fall head over heels with him after all.'

The morning after, Honoria had gone for a walk before breakfast, in much better spirits. As she came up the steps to re-enter by the breakfast room, she carelessly caught her new French muslin (fifteen and sixpence the yard, Mama had told her) on the roses that grew on a column. If she took her time and did not pull, she may be able to rescue herself without damage to the dress. She could hear Mama and Papa chatting and gave it no mind until Mama's voice became serious.

'My dear Ranalph, will you not tell me?'

'Shall there be muffins this morning, my dear?' said Papa cheerfully.

'You did not finish your mutton last night and you are falsely cheerful this morning. Tell me, my love.'

'You should apply for a position at Bow Street, my dear. Nothing escapes you.' She heard the sound of an embrace.

'Diversionary tactics, sir, are futile.'

Honoria knew she should not be privy to this, but she was still detaching her dress, thorn by thorn. It was incumbent on her to make a noise, so that they might know she was there, but as she decided to do so, she was frozen by Papa's next words.

'Mr Allison's visit will resolve all, I'm sure.'

Honoria closed her mouth, automatically continuing to silently pluck her dress from the rose bush, anxious to be away.

'Resolve what, dearest?' Honoria could picture her mama on Papa's knee.

'Well, there have been extra expenses – from the Brighton property.' Honoria knew that this was where her uncle Wilbert lived, her father's younger brother. (Dickie had explained that he was a friend of the Prince Regent, which sounded so well to the girls, but Dickie had shaken his head loftily. 'You girls know nothing. Unless you are as rich as a Maharajah, it's ruinous to be part of that set.')

Her father continued, 'Now, now. All is well. If things do not take with Mr Allison, we shall just have to cut our cloth a little, Madame.' He breathed. 'But, Cynthia, I'm afraid another London Season is not to be thought of.'

Honoria felt instant guilt. Her own season had been at a rather later age than that of her more prosperous friends, and she had not been able to understand why Serena and she could not have had it together, for they borrowed each other's clothes all the time. Serena's intrepid spirit would have buoyed hers too and made her laugh, and would have surely helped with her crippling timidity. But when she had seen how many dresses had been required - one day alone she had changed from morning gown to carriage dress to luncheon half dress, then riding habit and finally evening dress. And with so many of the same people at balls, one could not make do - Mama had insisted on twenty evening gowns as the bare minimum. However doughty with a needle the sisters might be, this was beyond their scope, and London dressmakers did not come cheap. Two such wardrobes were not to be paid for by the estate's income in one year. Honoria had accidentally seen the milliner's bill for her season and shuddered to think of it - her bonnets alone had been ruinously expensive. She had looked forward to her second season, where her wardrobe could be adapted at very little cost to give it a new look and Serena would also have her fill of new walking dresses and riding habits, bonnets and stockings. If she were in London with her sister, she might actually enjoy it.

'Poor Serena. What are her chances of a suitable match in this restricted neighbourhood?' Mama continued, 'And indeed, Honoria, if she does not like this match. Though how she could fail to like a charming, handsome man like Mr Allison is beyond me,' she finished.

'Do not forget rich,' teased her husband.

'When I think of the girls who tried to catch him all season! And then he came to us – specifically asked to be presented to her as a partner for the waltz, as dear Lady Carlisle informed me later - but she showed no triumph at all. And now, she will not give an opinion. She is strangely reticent about the subject.'

'Well, well, it is no doubt her shyness. She will be more relaxed when she sees Allison among the family.'

'So much rests upon it.' There was a pause. 'Dickie's commission?'

He laughed, but it sounded sour from her always cheerful Papa. 'Wilbert has promised to buy it from his next win at Faro.'

'Hah!' said Mama bitterly.

Honoria was free. She went towards the breakfast room rather noisily.

'Are there muffins?' she asked gaily.

'How on earth do you come to be engaged to *him*?'

Honoria was jolted back to the present by Serena's outcry. She gazed in dread over her sister's dark curls and saw a sober figure in a black coat and dull breeches, with a wide-brimmed, antediluvian hat walking towards the house. She gave an involuntary giggle.

'Oh, that is only Mr Scribster, his friend.'

'*He* you remember!' laughed Serena. 'Is he as dull as his hat?'

Honoria remembered Mr Scribster's long, miserable face, framed with two lank curtains of hair, at several parties. She thought it odd that a gentleman so patently uninterested in the events should bother to attend. And indeed her mother had whispered the same to her. Honoria must be present where her parents willed her - but surely a gentleman should be free not to? But Mr. Scribster attended in company with Lord Salcomb or Mr Allison with a face suitable for a wake.

'Yes,' said Honoria. 'He never looks happy to be anywhere. And generally converses with no one. Though occasionally I saw him speak to Mr Allison in his grave way and Mr. Allison *laughed*.'

'Maybe it's like when Sir Henry Horton comes to dinner.' Sir Henry was nicknamed among the children "The Harbinger of Gloom". 'Papa laughs so much at his doomsday declarations that he is the only man in the county that actually looks forward to him coming.'

Honoria spotted another man exiting the chaise, this one in biscuit coloured breeches above shiny white-topped Hessian boots. His travelling coat almost swept the ground, and

Serena said, 'Well, he's more the thing at any rate. Pity we cannot see his face. You should be prepared. However, he *walks* like a handsome man.' She giggled, 'Or at all events, a rich one.'

The door behind them had opened. 'Serena, you will guard your tongue,' said their mama. Lady Fenton, also known as Lady Cynthia (as she was the daughter of a peer) was the pattern card from which her beautiful daughters were formed. A dark-haired, plump, but stylish matron who looked as good as one could, she said of herself, when one had borne seven bouncing babies. Now she smiled, though, and Honoria felt another bar in her cage. How could she dash her mother's hopes? 'Straighten your dresses, girls, and come downstairs.'

Benedict winked and walked off with his parent.

There were no looking glasses in their bedroom, so as not to foster vanity. But as they straightened the ribbons of the new dresses Mama had thought appropriate to the occasion, they acted as each other's glass and pulled at hair ribbons and curls as need be. The Misses Fenton looked as close to twins as sisters separated by two years could, dark curls and dark slanted eyes and lips that curled at the corners to give them the appearance of a smile even in repose. Their brother Benedict said they resembled a couple of cats, but then he would say that. Serena had told him to watch his tongue or they might scratch.

The children, Norman, Edward, Cedric and Angelica, were not to be admitted to the drawing room - but they bowled out of the nursery to watch the sisters descend the stairs in state. As Serena tripped on a cricket ball, she looked back and stuck her tongue out at the grinning eight-year-old Cedric. Edward, ten, cuffed his younger brother and threw him into the nursery by the scruff of his neck. The eldest, Norman, twelve, a beefy chap, lifted little three-year-old Angelica who showed a disposition to follow her sisters. On the matter of unruly behaviour today, Mama had them all warned.

As the stairs turned on the landing, the sisters realised there was no one in the large square hall to see their dignified descent, so Serena tripped down excitedly, whilst her sister made the slow march of a hearse follower. As Serena gestured her down, Honoria knew that her sister's excitement came from a lack of society in their neighbourhood. She herself had enjoyed a London season, whilst Serena had never been further than Harrogate. She was down at last and they walked to the door of the salon, where she shot her hand out to delay Serena. She took a breath and squared her shoulders. Oh well, this time she should at least see what he looked like.

Two gentlemen stood by the fire with their backs to the door, conversing with Papa and Dickie. As the door opened, they turned and Honoria was focused on the square-shouldered gentleman, whose height rivalled Benedict's and quite dwarfed her sturdy papa. His face was nearly in view, Sir Ranalph was saying, 'These are my precious jewels!' The face was visible for only a moment before Serena gave a yelp of surprise and moved forward a pace. Honoria turned to her.

'But it's you!' Serena cried.

Everyone looked confused and a little shocked, not least Serena who grasped her hands in front of her and regarded the carpet. There seemed to be no doubt that she had addressed Mr Allison.

Honoria could see him now, the dimpled chin and strong jaw she remembered, and topped by a classical nose, deep set hazel eyes and the hairstyle of a Roman Emperor. Admirable, she supposed, but with a smile dying on his lips, he had turned from relaxed guest to stuffed animal, with only his eyes moving between one sister and another. His gaze fell, and he said the most peculiar thing.

'Blue slippers.'

Made in the USA
Columbia, SC
25 March 2023